WHITE TRASH GOTHIC 3

EDWARD LEE

DEADITE PRESS
833 SE Main Street #342
Portland, OR 97214
www.DEADITEPRESS.com

AN ERASERHEAD PRESS COMPANY
www.ERASERHEADPRESS.com

ISBN: 978-1-62105-326-2

DEDICATION

For Dallas Mayr, GAK and Charlee Jacob. Rest in peace.

ACKNOWLEDGMENTS

Christine Morgan, Dave Barnett, Liz & Suze, Jackie Mitchell, Samia, Bob Hinton, Mike Ling, Babaganoosh, Dustin LaValley, Ellie Gibbons, Kyle Nonneman, Becky Narron, Will Skaar, Kylie the Cremator, Carolyn Young, Lisa, Kristy A Hucul, Mike Hanusch, Marc Schnieder, Robb Chavers, Jonathan Grisham, Artem Ageev, Tammi Rotolo, Trevor Justin Bailey, Zubin Garda, John Baltisberger, Paul McGee from Liverpool, Annika Liu and Heike, Hunter Rinier, Anthony Michalos, James Walker, Branden Fisher, Duilio Cerini, Jonathan Mayon, Thomas K. Smith, Haden Glock, Mark Watts, Ashley E. Davis, James and Gigi, Roman Neznau, Gray, Tony Kendall, and Lisa Ille who got an Edward Lee tattoo!

WHITE TRASH GOTHIC SAGA by EDWARD LEE:

WHITE TRASH GOTHIC 3

LAST TIME: I'll ask the reader to carry her or his mind back to the end of Part 2 of this gallivanting and rather untamed redneck saga. The Bighead is on the loose, having been resuscitated not long ago by the Writer's mysterious doppelganger. For reasons good or evil, we don't yet know, though it's difficult to reckon how anything good could lay at the roots of re-infusing the blood supply of a legendary walking slaughterhouse into its nine-foot-long corpse and subsequently raising it from the dead. And as for the genetic provenance of the Bighead, we know very little. We know that he is a hybrid, and we know that one part of that hybrid is human. But what of the other part? The tales of old wives, etc., suggest that Bighead is also part *demon,* other tales tell us he is part *alien.* The world may never know...

Now let us recall, too, the convoluted and undeniably nebulous "mission" of the Writer and his two promiscuous companions, Snowie and Dawn. Both of these late-twentysomethings are conveniently equipped with, shall we say, *Brick Fuckin' Shit House* bodies that would make a celibate monk howl at the moon, and their mammarian endowments existed in a condition that could only be described as that of unadulterated perfection. But...enough about their sexual attributes. Snowie possessed an unparalleled uniqueness–er, *two* such uniquenesses, I should point out. One, she was an albino, covered overall with stunning paper-white skin which sometimes betrayed the faintest touch of pink, and the hair atop her head was a shimmering sprawl of crinkly off-white (a trait shared by the hair of a certain area *lower* than her head). Ah, but the second uniqueness was just this: not only was she an albino with a *very* provocative body, she was a distant blood-relative of none other than the famous academic horror writer H.P. Lovecraft. How came this, you ask, as we're told that Lovecraft fathered no children? It's a long story, which can be found in detail in the novella entitled *Pages Torn from a Travel Journal* by Edward Lee (and available now on Amazon!) It will have to do to say only that in the late-1920s, while on one of his many bus tours of America, Mr. Lovecraft's bus was delayed for a day thanks to mechanical difficulties, and was forced to stop for repairs in–yes!–Luntville. During the night, after much to-do, Mr. Lovecraft's sperm found its way into the vagina of a promiscuous local albino woman. The rest is history. The progeny of this very fortunate woman branched out tentacularly throughout the region and always kept dominant the albinism gene as well certain genes belonging to Mr. Lovecraft. The physical result? Every single descendant of this albino woman, no matter how remote, is in distinct possession of the facial structure of H.P. Lovecraft: a long, narrow face with an over-protuberant jaw. As for Snowie in particular, try to imagine Lovecraft's head situated on the neck of, say, Raquel Welch in *One Million Years B.C.* How's *that* for an image?

And now we move on to our second female lead, Dawn, who boasts a body and pair of breasts just as awesome as Snowie's. She's a bit shorter and plusher and has shining shoulder-length brown hair and keen, dark eyes. (I don't remember her last name, nor am I willing to go back to Book 1 to find out.) She is a disabled U.S. Army veteran, and while gallantly serving her country in some shithole corner of the Middle East, she lost one leg from the knee down in a mishap with an improvised explosive device. (I don't remember which leg it was, nor am I willing to go back to Book 1 to find out.) She also holds a fascinating occupational credential. In the Army she was a trained Combat Mortuary Specialist; she would perform field autopsies on coalition decedents and dead enemy combatants. (And with these latter, she became quite skilled with the portable embalming machine. You see, if the corpse was "fresh" enough, an unauthorized alteration of the embalming process made it possible to, in a word, "erect" the dead. In other words, Dawn produced many a raging boner on many a dead terrorist, and she and her female soldier friends made darn good use of those boners. Ah, but I've said enough on this topic.)

What else have we in this brief introductory recap? Oh, yes. The Writer's mysterious "mission." He, Dawn, and Snowie have deputed themselves the to mansion of the long-dead resident Ephriam Crafter, who was thought by many to be a modern-day warlock. After having arrived, the Writer and his companions are surprised to encounter a visitor, an African American man dressed in black who calls himself "Case." You may recall way back in Edward Lee's disgraceful novel *Header 2* a sociopathic homicidal heroin dealer with the same name, and the two Cases are indeed the same man. But Case is no longer a "smack-slinger;" he is instead a full-fledged "born-again" Christian who has turned from the error of his ways in order to repent. He now exists to serve God, and he works, rather under the table, for the Catholic Church, sort of their private investigator, sent to look into things that the Church prefers not to acknowledge formally, like demons, exorcisms, paranormality, and the like. Furthermore, Case is touched periodically by genuine psychic talents, which come in handy (especially for a sloppy and often haphazard writer). But at this precise moment–you may be asking– just where *is* Case?

You'll have to wait a short while, I'm afraid, for the answer to that question.

You see, the Writer and Case have seen fit to DIG UP the grave of Ephriam Crafter, and guided by instructions provided by a stolen vellum page of the infamous Voynich manuscript and further instructions that had been tattooed on the *back* of Crafter's corpse, have been made privy to a revelation. The cryptic combination of instructions revealed to the two men exactly how to open one of the wood-plank doors in Crafter's basement, and they had it on good occult authority that these doors were actually things called "traversion bridles," which are, in essence, *doors to Hell.*

If you'll excuse me, I must now catch my breath.

There.

Where were we? Yes! The Writer and Case have discerned, via their mutual metaphysical studies, that these bridles require a *human sacrifice* in order to open them, and the particulars of that sacrifice are thus: a *living person* must be impaled through the heart on one of the iron spikes which jut from the center of each door. Of course, neither man is capable of the deed– cold-blooded murder–but wouldn't you know it? At just that moment, a previously mentioned minor character–one Pastor Tommy Ignatius–joins the Writer and Case in the basement. Pastor Tommy is a television evangelist. He is quite famous and quite wealthy. He is also, like many television evangelists, quite a fraud and quite a sexual pervert. His perversions, in fact, tread well past felonious boundaries. For instance, while in the privacy of his own room, he indulges in that unspeakable human disgrace and outrage, that of catering to child pornography. And while watching this stuff, we learn that he also has a penchant for a type of candy called Gummy Worms but...he doesn't eat them, he...does something else with them. Anyway, not a moment or two after Pastor Tommy steps into the Crafter basement, *another figure* rushes down the steps, bursts into the room, knocks down the Writer and Case, and then slams Pastor Tommy against one of the spiked doors. This act, of course, impales the pastor's heart on the spike, which (you guessed it) activates the "traversion bridle," and the wooden door farthest to the right swings open.

Remember now, this is a door to HELL.

And with this, the unidentified murderer of Pastor Tommy darts into that door and disappears.

The Writer does not see exactly what happened when he was knocked down, but Case does. Case, in fact, is able to identify the surprise intruder at once: none other than the reanimated corpse of Ephriam Crafter!

Next, Case does the least logical thing: convinced it is his duty to God, he, too, rushes through the open door and disappears.

The Writer now stands alone in the satanic basement, looking at a wide-open door to Hell. In the next moment, he is up the stairs, moving faster than he'd ever moved in his life.

The project of deciding what to do next is a daunting one indeed. But he guesses that finding Snowie and Dawn would be a good start. Previously, perhaps an hour ago, they'd both come into the house to take showers, and the Writer became reasonably agitated when hearing the shower running in a nearby room. There was no time for lollygagging, and knowing those two, in the shower together, there would likely be *quite a bit* of lollygagging. *It doesn't take this long to take a shower!* comes the fuming thought, but just before he would barge in and yell at them, he is signaled from behind by the voices of two women.

It is Snowie and Dawn who stood behind him, both already showered and dressed. This leaves an interesting question: if they're both standing behind him right now, then *who* is in the shower?

The Writer has had enough surprises today but whether he likes it or not, one more awaits.

He walks into the bathroom whence the shower noise comes. At that second the water is turned off, and a lean, tanned, and very curious looking nude woman steps out of the shower. She has a bit of a "wild" look, which causes the Writer to wonder if she is a local hill girl or "creeker," as they are called. Her dark hair clearly hasn't been cut in years or decades; it hangs past her knees.

Eventually, she identifies herself as Charity Wells, and says further, "I'm the Bighead's twin sister."

How's that for a cliffhanger?

And if you don't know who Charity Wells is, then you haven't read the very first novel in this saga, and that novel would be *The Bighead* by Edward Lee. Fortunately, however, it is not absolutely necessary for you to have read it, so skilled is the author of this book at the process of story telling!

Anyway, so much for our refresher-course of Book 2. Now, let us find ourselves at the first page of Book 3...

* * *

Ah, there. And now that we're settled comfortably on the first page, we're thrown for a bit of a loop. We might reasonably expect that Book 3 would commence immediately where Book 2 ended; i.e., the Writer dumbfounded as he stands in a first-floor bathroom of the Crafter house, having just discovered a mysterious naked woman named Charity Wells. Yes, that would be the logical place to start, and for that reason, and that reason alone, we *won't* start there.

We'll start, instead, in Whitesburg, Kentucky, a tiny, blip-on-the-map town in the southeastern part of the state. Not two thousand people reside there, and little exists to attract tourists, unless one considers a marching band competition and a "public art" park to be features worthy of notice. It is quaint, inconspicuous, and quiet, a town still retaining a touch of the Good Old Days, and old-fashioned ideas like patriotism, God and Country, and traditional family values. Crime is near-non-existent, and drug use is nil. Everyone helps their neighbor, and everyone knows everyone else. Whitesburg, as you might imagine, is the perfect place to raise a family.

It's also the perfect place to have a Mafia "snuff" house, which you very likely might *not* imagine.

"Are you shitting me, Augie? *That's* the kid?" asked the shortish man in the dark suit. He had dyed-black hair and a face that many would deem "weasely." His name was Paul "Paulie" Vinchetti III, and he was, for lack of a better term, "a Mob boss." Many of you know who he is. For those who don't, I can't only ask your pardon, because reciting Mr. Vinchetti's history and credentials here is a task that I simply cannot *bear* to repeat.

His query was answered, "Yeah, boss. That's the kid, all right," by a huge ox-like man at Paulie's side. This was Augie, the "lieutenant," you might say, Paulie's sergeant-at-arms. Anvil-faced, broad-shouldered, and six-foot-five, an Italian juggernaut.

The "kid" being referred to now was actually a newborn baby, and on the table before the two very evil men the baby lay in a little bassinet-type thing. It looked up at this pair of demented murderers, smiled giddily, and started making goo-goo-gaa-gaa noises.

"Fuck, Augie," Paulie pronounced, "ain't that a kick in the rocks? Kid's supposed to be all fucked-up lookin', and deformed and shit. Looks perfectly normal to me."

"Me too, boss."

Paulie smirked. "I mean, are you *sure?* Are you *sure* this kid's mother was that hype we fed nothin' but horse-sperm for nine-months?"

"Positive, boss," Augie guaranteed. "I watched it flop out her snatch, me and Tony Big Ears. We was filmin' it, of course. Shit, Tony—that dumb dago—he thought the kid was gonna have a horse head."

Paulie laughed hard—harder, perhaps, than the reference warranted—so Augie followed suit.

In all, it was an *adorable,* and *perfectly normal* baby, and it was grinning up at Paulie with spit bubbles, like he was its father.

"For fuck's sake, Augie. That kid's too cute ta, ta—you know..."

"Sure do, boss. Cutest little thing I ever seen, and it looks like he likes ya, thinks you're its pop."

"Fuck!" Paulie yelled. "And *what* are we supposed to do with this one? A wood-chipper job?"

"Yeah, boss."

"For that Irish hard-on in Union City, the plastic surgeon? One who said he'll pay twenty grand?"

"Naw, boss. It's for the sheenie dentist in Hoboken, said he'd pay thirty."

Paulie's morality clashed with his sense of commerce. Commerce usually won out. "Thirty large?" He grimaced at Augie. "You tell me, Augie. What kind of gutter-scum piece'a shit sick *fuck* would pay for a video clip of a cute little newborn baby bein' dropped in a fuckin' *wood-chipper?*"

"Beats me, boss. Sick in the head, lotta people are."

"And, sure, we've done stuff like that in the past a shitload of times, but, but..." Paulie looked back at the baby. "I mean, if it was a *fucked up* baby, like it was supposed to be, then that's different. Like way back when Bam Bam fire-bombed that school of retarded kids after chaining all the exits. Fuck. They were *retarded* kids, never woke up to a good day in their lives, didn't know shit from chocolate fuckin' mousse–we were doin' 'em a favor. And then, and then, remember that baby we steam-rolled on film upstate?"

"Aw, yeah, boss. Hard to forget that one. Mickey Big Ass was drivin' the rig."

"Yeah, yeah, and I don't feel bad about that 'cos, shit, that poor little munchkin didn't have no arms and legs. We was doin' him a favor."

"I think it was a girl, boss, but, yeah, we did her a favor. Wouldn't've had nothin' good in her life, so maybe she got a better shot in the next one."

"Yeah, yeah!" Paulie excitedly said.

"We helped the kid out and picked up twenty big ones

from that wog doctor in St. Louis. He was *real happy* with that clip. But Mickey Big Ass...not so much. The poor fat fuck couldn't eat for a week, and says he *still* has nightmares."

Paulie thoughtfully pinched his chin, like the Thinker at Columbia University. "You gotta wonder, Augie, don't ya? What do these rich guys *get* out of buyin' video clips of kids gettin' killed?"

"Don't know, boss. But the Doc—God rest his soul—always said it was something sexual—"

"Sexual?"

"Yeah, like some repressed shit goes back to their childhood. Said those kind'a guys couldn't get it up for regular shit, so they do this. Only way they can come, he said, by beatin' off watchin' kids and babies get mulched or tortured."

"That's fucked up, ain't it, Aug?"

"Sure is, boss."

Paulie bore an expression that suggested a conflict of resolve and a misery of doubt, something clean contrary to his demeanor. Then he said in a blurt, "Fuck it, Augie! I ain't gonna let this cute little baby get dropped in a chipper just so that sheenie dentist can bust a nut, and to hell with the thirty grand. We're all pig shit rich anyway. So fuck it. The deal's off with that matzah-ball-filled heeb *fuck* in Hoboken. My baby-killin' days are over. How's that sound, ya big goombah?"

Augie cut a giant grin. "Sound's *great,* boss. I guess we're both mellowin' with age."

"Yeah, tell me about it, shit." Paulie looked down at the baby again, delighted. "Better call Charlie M. and tell him and his crew ta drop the baby off at one'a them adoption lawyers. They can make him an offer he can't refuse."

"I'm on it, boss," Augie said, whipped out his cellphone, and began to happily oblige the command, split-infinitive be damned. (Sometimes, it just sounds better, damn it.)

Paulie poured himself a shot of Johnny Red neat and

downed it just as Augie finished his call. "So what else is on the schedule today, Aug? Anything?"

"Well, yeah. Jimmy Limp Dick and his boys nabbed that federal judge in D.C. who had the balls to use your name in a congressional hearing about organized crime."

Paulie hooted. "Well, holy *fuck*, Augie. I want that judge's *ass*! Please tell me they didn't ice the guy!"

"They didn't ice the guy, boss. And better yet, it ain't a guy—"

"Huh? Ya mean the judge is a *chick?*"

Augie's very big, angular-jawed head nodded, and his expression took on a cast of something like reserved excitement. "The judge is a chick, all right, boss, and you ready for the best part? She's a looker. Check out this pic Jimmy just texted me—"

Augie shared the jpeg on his smartphone, and Paulie immediately squeezed his own crotch. The woman in the jpeg was indeed a looker...even with the two black eyes, broken teeth, and at least one missing ear. She'd been gagged, then tied down to one of those spinal boards that EMTs used. Nude, of course, and was that a hard human bitemark over one nipple? She was probably pushing fifty, but this Harvard-educated bitch wore those years well and had spent most of them exercising and eating right. She wanted to look good sitting up there on the federal bench when she was condemning good Italian brothers to life without parole. Paulie was already sporting a bit of wood from the image. The judge had been belted to the board from neck to waist, leaving the creamy athletic legs hanging sprawled, and the outflow of semen evident at her crotch—a completely bald snatch, mind you—indicated without dispute that Jimmy's crew had already taken some hearty liberties with the meat and potatoes of her womanhood.

"Fuck, Augie," Paulie instructed. "Make sure they don't kill her before I get to see her. That's a prime piece of ass if I ever saw one, and I might need to make a deposit before we send her out the chimney."

Augie nodded, arms crossed. "Yeah, boss, I figured you'd wanna do a special job on her, so I told Jimmy not to snuff her or fuck her up too much. Said we'd meet him in Luntville at the gimp's funeral parlor."

"Perfect," Paulie beamed, still rubbing his crotch.

"But first we gotta decide what to do with the mother."

"What mother?"

"The baby's mother, you know, the hype we knocked up'n fed nothin' but horse cum for nine months."

Paulie nodded. "Oh, *that* mother, yeah. Well, what d'you think we should do with her?"

Augie shrugged. "Well, we can let her go but she can't move 'cos the Doc cut all her tendons and nerves'n shit. Or we can get some log boys in here to knock her up again, then feed her nothin' but horse cum for another nine months. Or..." Augie's huge shoulders shrugged. "We can have Tony drop her in the wood-chipper."

Paulie mulled over the possibilities. Would his newfound sense of mercy strike again?

(We pause for a dramatic effect.)

No.

"Drop that dirty hype in the wood-chipper," Paulie said. "Better yet, lower her in *slow.*"

* * * *

Fuck, thought the Writer, and it seemed like a particularly appropriate thought. Here he stood, in the open doorway of the first floor bathroom of the Crafter mansion, watching the very wild-looking woman named Charity Wells finish drying her lean, toned, tanned body after what she'd claimed to be her first shower in twenty years.

She'd made an additional claim as well, remember: that she was the Bighead's twin sister. The prospect of *that* made for a very interesting amalgamation of genes. But the Writer's thoughts had no time to stray, nor could he allow himself to keep staring at Charity's tanned breasts. There was serious business afoot: the Bighead was on the loose, probably slaughtering people en masse, Case was in Hell, and downstairs, a door to the Netherworld stood wide open. The Writer could hazard not even an inkling of a guess as to what his next move should be.

Instead, after wrapping the towel around herself, it was Charity who spoke. "I remember when I was staying at my aunt's boarding house, she told me a few stories about this house, *weird* stories. Like it's cursed or something."

"More than cursed," offered the Writer. "The owner was a sorcerer of some repute, if you believe in that sort of thing."

"Do you?" Charity asked.

The Writer, Snowie, and Dawn all said "Yes," at the same time, and then the Writer continued, "There's a satanic temple down in the basement, which I know sounds absurd. At any rate, one of our friends disappeared into it."

Charity stared in amused curiosity. "Your friend... *disappeared* into a temple, that's in the basement?"

"A *door* in the temple, I should say. The short version is this: a certain occult accident occurred, and one of the temple doors opened. And our friend–his name is Case–he went through that door. According to some ancient grimoires, that door leads into some unspecified sector of Hell."

Charity's bare, tanned shoulders shrugged. "Hell, huh? So when's he going to come out?"

The Writer's voice faltered. "I can't even estimate. I've been too afraid to go back down there. I don't even know if Case *can* come back out, and I don't know if the door's still open."

Charity's eyes thinned. "Well, why don't we go look?"

"Or how's 'bout this?" Snowie asserted. "Forget about this Case fella, and let's just go on home."

Dawn hitched her massive braless breasts up under her Army t-shirt. "Yeah. Fuck Case. We don't know that guy from shit."

"Girls," said the Writer. "The man just saved both of you from a demonic possession."

"Blah, blah, blah," Dawn replied. "Fuck Case, and fuck this fucked up, creepy fuckin' house. Let's leave, let's go home."

It looked like a very unpleasant situation was about to commence but luckily Charity interceded with these words, "But before you do that, it really can't hurt to go down to the basement real quick and check the door, right?"

* * * *

Only a few miles away, over a hill or two and a dale or two—wait a minute. What exactly *is* a dale? (A negligible pause.) Ah, I see it means *valley.* Anyway, in a region not terribly distant from our protagonists and their current situation at the cursed Crafter house, there stretched a tract of land owned and maintained by the county department of education, comprised of enough acreage to facilitate two intramural-sized baseball fields with backstops and benches and, in between, an additional perimeter which served as a football field and also a soccer field, depending on the season. An auxiliary segment of land existed at the back-end of this perimeter; this served as an overflow lot for various county vehicles either not currently in use, or awaiting replacement or repair, and was sparsely occupied now by several snow plows, one school bus, and some tractors. Now, the author apologizes for the dullness of this passage, but he begs your attention to one last detail, since it's an *important* one. Given the regrettable propensity some persons have to take what's not theirs, especially easily siphoned gasoline, a well-set ten-foot-high chainlink fence circumscribed the entirety of this perimeter, not just the overflow lot but also the baseball diamonds, bleachers, and the soccer/football field.

It is my hope that the creatively enterprising reader will now wonder what could possibly be *important* about a run-of-the-mill chainlink fence. Hmm? Feel free to regard this as something of a hint...

The fence gate had been unlocked early that morning by a county employee of long-standing, a ramshackle, middle-aged man named Rud Gooder, and it was into that vast fenced compound that Rud had driven the school first-aid van, painted white, of course, with a big red cross on it, plus a sign that read WATER STATION. A great deal of the van was populated by a cot, some medical equipment, and a bunch of first aid kits, while a more forward section hosted long coolers filled with ice and bottled water, and a flip-door Good Humor truck sort of opening from which Rud could pass bottles of water to anyone who requested it. Today was the first day of varsity and junior varsity high school girl's soccer tryouts, and before long this area would be bustling with more than a few dozen energetic high school girls looking to compete for places on the teams. Many parents would also attend, as spectators, and of course the team managers and coaches.

Nurse Cutler arrived by 9 a.m.: early '40s, apple-sized tits, and a big shapely butt which did a magnificent job of stretching out her white, mid-thigh nurse's dress. Silken light-red hair danced at her shoulders. Great-looking, yes, and many, many other male persons at the school had cranked out many a load of sperm thinking about her. Yet the look in her eyes was mostly a knife-sharp glare that said I HATE ALL MEN, and her attitude companioned that look very well.

High falutin cunt, Rud thought when she arrived. *Bet my ass her favorite game show is Truth Or CUNT-sequences, and I'll bet she was born and raised in CUNTington, West Virginia! Oh, how I would love to punch her in the face and kick her in the pussy—over and over and over again. Shit. If she was a puppy she'd sure as hell be the CUNT of the litter!*

When she came inside the van, she immediately smirked and said with no geniality, "Good morning, Mr. Gooder. It's going to be a very hot day, as I'm sure you know since I'm sure you checked the weather earlier. We can't risk dehydration and heat-stroke, can we? We have to look out for our girls, don't we? I'm sure we'll need at least 200 bottles of water."

"We got a hundred or so," Rud said back. "Like always. You stick ta your job, and I'll stick ta mine."

"Fine, Mr. Gooder," she replied with the faintest smile. "And if you run out of water, you can be sure I'll put it in my report."

Go ahead and put it in your report, and I'll go ahead and put my foot up your ass and kick up your last meal, which was probably alfalfa sprouts, soybean hot dogs, and vegetarian cheese. No, Rud didn't like this snooty man-hating bitch one bit, as she was always diligent about asserting her authority over him. *What were those things called back in the olden colonial days?* he asked himself. *You know, the things they punished criminals in? They lock your neck and wrists down in notches in a wooden crossbeam? A pillory? Yeah, that's it! I'd like ta lock down this huffy bitch in a fuckin' PILLORY and piss on her head every day and jerk off on her hair and lather the shit up like Dippity Doo, then go around behind, ass-fuck her, and then kick her in the pussy, over and over and over, until it got all swole up like a big ole hot water bag, yes sir!*

Anyway, these are the thoughts that Rud's brain generated upon Nurse Cutler's arrival, and they painted a more than accurate picture of his opinion of her. Fortunately, all those cute high school girls began to arrive shortly thereafter and soon Rud had something far more positive to think about. He looked out his little service window with a knowing smile and watched the field fill up with gaiety and the revel of youth.

The coaches—all women themselves, and a few of them lookers—separated the girls into their class groups, lined them up, and began to teach the fundamentals of soccer. There came the sound of balls being kicked, whistles blowing, sneakers trampling, and dozens of high school girls shrieking and laughing in competitive, athletic glee. The students all wore rather tight white shorts, knee-high white socks and white sneakers, along with white numbered tunics, and the coaches had them practicing various soccer drills, passing exercises, kicking techniques and other things that Rud–and no doubt the reader as well–have virtually no interest in.

As all those young girls celebrated their wondrous youth and athletic abilities, Rud reveled deeply in the luxury of his own musings, which involved all manner of perverted sexual contact with the ladies of the field. The girls' ages ranged mainly from fifteen to eighteen, and we won't concern ourselves with the precise details of Rud's fantasies involving the majority of the girls who were seventeen and younger–hence, still minors. Ah, but a fair number of the seniors were eighteen and, damn it, they were fair game. Rud imagined all of them, first this instant, stripping naked right then and there.

What a sight that would be! Rud considered. *Especially during the warm-up exercises! Jumping jacks, deep knee bends– oh–and sit ups! All buck naked, all that young perfect skin shining with sweat, tits gleaming! Fuck!*

There were even several girls who were nineteen and twenty, delinquent give-a-shit hosebags who'd flunked a grade or two, and their parents had the good sense to force them to stay in 'til they got their diplomas.

Bunch of dopes, ain't good for nothin' 'cept smokin' the pot and fuckin' any swingin' dick that comes her way. Of course, Rud had dropped out of school in eighth grade, but the hypocrisy of his reflections didn't count. Why? Because he was a man, of course! *Men rule this world, not these trampy splittails!* And he would show them all if he could.

Like this huffy cunt right here, stalking up to the van with tits sticking out 'til next Tuesday. Teddi Dishman, her name was, and she might have even been twenty, so many times had the bitch flunked. Any time she might pass him in the school, she'd make a face like she was about to throw up, and then rub the inside corner of her eye with her middle finger. How do you like that shit, huh? Working class guy like Rud has to take shit like that from the likes of her just because he was a glorified janitor. *You'll get yours one day, cunt,* he thought, and that's when she walked right up to his little service window and said, "Gimme a water, ya old loser."

Rud stared at her, and in his mind pictured many delightful things that he'd like to do to Teddi Dishman. Just the other night he'd been surfing porn in his squalid apartment and came upon a bondage clip which boasted a trussed up big-tit bitch hanging off a post. Each enormous breast had been encircled by some stout rope and then twisted up so tight that they ballooned out from the sheer pressure, first displaying earthworm like veins beneath the skin, and then turning purple from the circulation being cut off.

Rud nodded in self satisfaction. *That's what I'd love to do to Teddi Dishman but also get another rope around her neck and twist that down too, till her face turned the same purple, and then jerk a nut off on her...*

"You deaf, ya old fuck?" said Teddi Dishman. "I said gimme a water."

So much for the tourniquet fantasy, but as Rud bent down to get a bottle of water, Nurse Cutler stepped out of her nurse cubby and said quite sternly, "Miss Dishman, talk like that is completely unacceptable. Mr. Gooder is your elder and he deserves your respect."

Teddi Dishman gave a jolt of surprise, clearly having been unaware of the nurse's presence until just now. "Yes, Nurse Cutler. I'm sorry, Nurse Cutler."

"Now you apologize to Mr. Gooder right this instant, or I'll report you to the principal."

Automaton-like, Teddi turned toward Rud. "I'm sorry, Mr. Gooder. I didn't mean it."

Rud stood duped. *I don't fuckin' believe it. Hacksaw Cutler just made that tit-wagon apologize to me!*

"Good girl," the nurse said. "Now take your water and run along."

"Yes, Nurse Cutler."

Nurse Cutler smiled, but it was a treacherous smile, and as she did so, she did this: she winked at Teddi. And Rud easily noticed that.

What a pair of cunting whores! It's a gawd-dag CUNT-spiracy! Rud thought.

Teddi Dishman grinned quickly up at Rud, began to turn back toward the field, and just before she would run off, she rubbed the inside corner of her eye with her middle finger.

No, this was not looking like it was going to be a good day for Rud. He just stood there bubbling while Nurse Cutler, with a pursing look of self-gratification, navigated her big shapely ass back into her nurse cubby, and began blipping on her cell-phone.

Rud looked back out into the field, at all those pretty athletic girls running around, kicking soccer balls, etc., but the enthusiasm for Rud had been all drained out of it now. *I'm stuck right smack-dab in the middle of a world of cunts.* Indeed, it looked like the only thing he'd have to get him through the day was his dick-hardening hatred. *Yeah, the World of Cunts, having a go at the old janitor, having a good girlie belly laugh, yes sir, a great big laugh on me. And, there—the ringleader. Nurse CUNTler.*

Well, they could take his dignity but they sure couldn't take his imagination, and right now Rud was imagining a hum-dinger of a fantasy: he'd locked both those bitches up in pillories, stripped naked, pulled a giant beer piss on both their heads, and then went around behind and had a good long kicking drill of his own, kicking their smug pussies for minutes, hours, days.

What a luxurious fantasy for good ole Rud Gooder!

As the day drew on, he caught himself peering, not at all

those sweating, bobbing, running high school girls but at the top of a distant hill.

Rud squinted. *What the hail? Is that a tree up there? But there weren't no tree up there before, was there? Naw, I don't think so...*

He was right. It wasn't a tree. What had snagged Rud's attention was nothing less than a figure, a *person*, yes, a person standing right up there on the top of the hill.

* * * *

"Ladies first?" the Writer offered just before the door that led down to the basement.

"Fuck off," Dawn said, which was the expected reply. Though the Writer might not be quite what one would call a profile in courage, he wasn't a coward, either. But right now?

I don't want to go down those stairs. I'm afraid...

"Come on, let's go," Charity said. "There's probably nothing there, it was probably your imagination."

No, it wasn't, the Writer thought and opened the door.

First thing noticeable was the large cross on the inside of the door. *Inside,* the Writer reminded himself, *to prevent anything unholy from escaping the basement.* The four of them descended then, the Writer in the lead, Charity right behind him, and Dawn and Snowie at the back, hugging each other. This time the Writer had brought the pistol he'd found in the car the other day, the big Webley .455. He didn't know about guns, and about the only thing he knew about *this* gun was that it was loaded, but who knew if the ancient ammunition was still functional? He didn't even know where the safety was. Charity said, "Yuck. What's that–"

"–smell?" Dawn finished.

The Writer noticed it full well. An odor like rotten eggs. "Sulphur, I do believe."

When the party made it to the bottom of the steps, they paused, then turned left and walked into the basement.

The far door of the traversion bridle remained standing open. The odor rose to a nearly noxious degree, along with other less-pleasant organic odors, like rotten meat, dead fish in the sun, bum B.O., and vomit and feces.

"Aw, fuuuuuuck this place!" Snowie complained. "I cain't stay here!" and then she thumped back up the stairs.

Dark, faint lights seemed to throb in the open doorway. The Writer edged closer, pistol in lead.

"So what happened exactly?" Charity asked. "This friend of yours went into that door? And its supposed to be *Hell* in there?"

The Writer gulped. "According to the ancient texts. And it's looking to me like it's not bullshit."

"But why on Earth would he do that?"

"I really have no idea."

"Well, if that door really does lead to Hell, what's to keep something that lives in *there* from coming out *here?*"

"Believe me," the Writer said. "I've considered that, but if I close the door, then Case might not ever be able to get back out."

Dawn chuckled. "Sounds like we need a search and rescue operation, but guess what? You can count me *out.*"

"Me too," but the Writer reflected. "I need to at least stick my head in, or go in a little ways, just to see if I can see anything."

"Bad idea," Charity said.

"Yeah," Dawn agreed, "you're out of your fucking mind. You go near that door, something could reach out and pull you in." Dawn paused to hitch her boobs up in the t-shirt; they must be getting rather uncomfortable in the rising heat and sulphur stink. "If something pulls you in, then me and Snowie will never get our new cars, and that would really suck."

"I appreciate your concern for my well-being," he said, but he did approach the door a few more steps so that he could look in.

He could see nothing but churning, dark-reddish light, felt more rank heat gust out, and heard, or thought he heard, imperceptible chatter, shrieks, moans, and witchlike laughter. This observation trebled his fear, but with it, something else trebled as well: his creative drive (*cre*ative, not *pro*creative). "I'm a writer, damn it! And a seer! It's my job to see as much in life as I can, and then *write* about it. Hell is through that door; therefore, I need to see Hell. So I can write about it! It's what I was put on Earth for! Don't you understand?"

"No," Dawn smirked. "If you're gonna be a dickhead enough to walk through the door then, please, at least give me your wallet and phone. You won't be needing those things in there, and you won't be coming back. Ever."

She's probably right, he thought, but then an idea occurred to him, because he was now in quite an intractable mood of insistence. "If I could figure out a way to hook my phone to a long stick, then I could turn on the video camera and stick it in the doorway like that."

"A really long selfie-stick, yeah," Dawn said. Then her eyes thinned. "Wait a minute! I can't believe I didn't think of it till now! Just like the Army! A drone!"

"A what?" Charity asked.

But the Writer thought he got it. *Drones, yeah.* Drones were in the news all the time now. Military use, law enforcement, even the Post Office was using them now to deliver packages... "I think I see what you mean."

"Good," Dawn said. "Let's get out of this stinking hot box and go back up and talk about this!"

They couldn't have evacuated the basement and its abyssal odor with any more promptitude, and not many minutes later a promising plan of action was decided upon as they all sat upstairs in the front parlor. To the Writer, it even sounded thrilling. He gave Dawn a sheaf of cash from his wallet, and she and Snowie would take the El Camino to the nearest town—a place called Tylersville—and proceed to a Blackwell Plaza which boasted, according to Dawn, a Radio Shack. "They sell all kinds of drones there, and they're not even expensive anymore." Furthermore, the drones were equipped with aerial cameras that could relay a live video feed back to a cell phone. The plan, in fact, was nearly ingenious. "We'll fly the drone into the door to Hell and see what it sees!" Dawn shrilled. Perhaps, they reckoned up, they might even find Case, and with any luck, he could follow the drone back to safety.

"It even sounds kinda like fun!" Snowie shared. "I'm kind'a curious what Hades' Place looks like!"

You and me both, thought the Writer.

Dawn and Snowie departed with their assignment, but not before they both hitched their big tits up beneath their shirts, and the Writer very much appreciated such incidental visions. *Does an old man good...* He'd previously instructed them to buy the best drone they could find, and they were also to buy food, some clothes for Charity, and, perhaps more crucial than anything, more beer, since the Writer was running low on his Collier's Civil War Lager.

The El Camino's huge 750 horse-power engine and chambered exhaust roared in the distance amid some impressive hole-shot-style rubber-burning, and then?

Silence returned, leaving the Writer and Charity Wells to sit alone in the blighted Crafter house.

Charity stretched out on a light purple Louis XV velvet sofa, her long tanned legs crossed erotically on the antique upholstery. She clearly felt no discomfort about being seen so casually by a perfect stranger—wrapped only in the towel—and hadn't cared in the least about being previously seen naked by him in the shower. The Writer could actually believe that she was indeed a wild woman living by herself in the woods; it was something about the vibe she gave off just lying there before him, lounging, looking up at the vaulted ceiling. He opened a bottle of beer, and said, "You're more than welcome to split this with me if you want. I can get a glass." He chuckled. "If I were more of a gentleman, I'd offer you the whole thing."

"Thanks but no," she said. "I never much cared for alcohol back in the day..."

"Back in the day, yes." The Writer saw this as an opening. He sat down on a tufted caramel leather ottoman and leaned forward to address her directly. "If you don't mind, that's what I'd like to talk about with you. Back in the days of your past. Earlier you implied that you'd been living in the wilds for around twenty years. It's hard for someone like me to understand how that's possible in this day and age. How do you eat? Where do you live?" He thought of the Wild Woman of Borneo and along those lines. "Are you really *naked* all the time?"

Charity laughed under her breath. "I'm naked most of the time, because it's more practical. Winter's another story, of course. But I do have some clothes. Campers and hikers sometimes forget jackets and things like that, lose things, leave things behind. Back when I took to the woods—"

"Twenty years ago?" the Writer pressed for clarification.

"I think so—something like that," she said. "When you live like I have for enough time, clocks and calenders stop having much meaning. In the beginning, when I first took to the woods, I did resort to theft sometimes. Campers were my targets mostly. I'd mostly steal clothes, food, tools, and money. Now, I don't feel good about that, but what the heck, huh? I was desperate, traumatized, and pretty messed up in the head." She smiled lazily at him. "This is a long story. You sure you want to hear it?"

"I need to hear it very much," the Writer nearly pleaded.

Charity Wells, then, told her story.

For most of the last twenty years, she'd lived quite successfully off the "grid." With tools either found, stolen, or purchased, she'd built a shelter for herself, a quite adequate shelter, which, she claimed, was about "ten feet square," and she'd built it deliberately right next to a spring well. Where, exactly? Near the Tug Fork State Nature Reserve. For the most part, she was a hunter-gatherer, and though she rarely ate game—such as squirrels, rabbits, and muskrat—the deep streams leading into the Tug Fork River (inaccessible to most campers and hikers) were teeming with fish, and if you knew how to make a spear and properly cut in a snag, there was no end to a quality protein source, plus the wild strawberries were as seemingly endless.

But wait a minute.

The Writer was fairly aware of the local geography, and he knew that the Tug Fork Reserve was on the Kentucky line, some forty miles distant. How had she traveled from there all the way to the Crafter house?

"I walked," came her nonchalant reply. "Got here in a little less than two days. Walking that far is no big deal if you're in shape and used to it."

Well, she was in shape, all right, as her well-toned muscles and super-low body fat index proved at a glance. "But why?" the Writer queried. "Why would you walk all that way just to come *here?*"

Again, she smiled. "I'm getting to that, and you're the one who asked, remember? You still want the whole story?"

"Sorry, yes. I *need* the whole story..."

So on it went.

Charity, claiming to be the Bighead's twin sister, was certain that she and her monstrous brother were connected by some sort of psychic tether—granted, a mild one, but a connection just the same. Even for the twenty years that the Bighead lay embalmed and "dead" in the Luntville Funeral Home, it wasn't totally dead, for aspects of its preternatural brain-matter still functioned a trifle.

Now that the unspeakable *thing* was up and about again, that psychic signal came through to Charity's perceptions loud and clear. And the message she was reading was *danger;* hence, she was led, for reasons unclear and cabalistic, to this nefarious house...

Then she went on to talk about more incidental things. She was a hermit living deep in the woods, yes, but she did have access to some creature comforts. All through the Tug Fork Forest Reserve as well as others could be found an abundance of ginseng plants, whose mature roots sold to roadside dealers for up to $500 a pound, and black and gold truffles, which grew all over the place, could bring in $100 a pound. So, when she needed more clothes, sandals, tools, or what have you, she could simply hike to the nearest town, and buy it. She'd even been known to buy charcoal, instant coffee, matches and lighters, various seasonings, etc. It hadn't taken long for her to realize how much more profoundly she preferred living on her own like this, than suffering the constant injustices and disappointments of living like everyone else in modern American society. Now she was free from the undue judgments of others and no longer subjected to societal expectations.

"I got a brand-new wonderful life the minute I wandered off the road all those years ago and disappeared into the woods."

"But how did you even learn that you were the Bighead's twin sister?" asked the Writer, who then took a chug of beer and watched her face and eyes.

"My Aunt Annie told me, shortly before she died. She was torn apart and partially eaten–"

"By the Bighead," the Writer said rather than asked.

"By the Bighead. But I already had an idea because the minute I got into town, to my aunt's boarding house, I started feeling that psychic vibe, that there was something awful out there that was connected to me."

The Writer maintained his angle of questioning, watching for facial tics, watching for any possible deceptive delays or behavioral tags that might indicate fabrication. "So did you ever see your twin brother? Did you ever meet him?"

Charity spared a laugh. "Yes, but *meet* isn't the word I'd use. At birth we were immediately separated so I only know what I was told about that."

"But what's to tell? Your mother gave birth to twins, right? Happens all the time."

"Yes, but what doesn't happen all the time is a mother giving birth to twins and one of them is a homicidal monster. The Bighead came out of my mother first–he was too big to come out properly, so he *ate* his way out. Of course, my mother died almost instantly. But then I came out of what was left of her."

"Fuck," the Writer muttered, trying to blot out the mental image.

"I do remember seeing him, on that last night before I took to the woods, the night that the Bighead raped me..."

Here the enthusiasms of the Writer's contemplations came to an abrupt halt. After Charity had said this, she seemed to be staring upward, eyes wide in a daze. *So that's what she meant when she'd said she was traumatized,* the Writer reasoned.

But was it true? Had she really been raped by the Bighead? This information advanced a considerable conflict.

Now Charity lay on her side, eyeing at him. "You look like you don't believe me. But don't worry. I'm not offended if you think I'm lying..."

"I wouldn't say I think you're lying," he said. "But what you say seriously contradicts a major component of the legend–that no woman can survive such an encounter. Many, many women have been raped by the Bighead, but none have survived, because–well, because..." Now the gentleman in the Writer panicked for a couth way to say the rest.

"Because," Charity said with a sly smile, "the Bighead's genitals are *huge.* When that thing gets hard, it's over two feet long–I don't care what anyone says, and it gets almost as big around as a coffee can." Her eyes narrowed as she looked at him with more intensity. "*Think* about that. Try to picture an erection *that big.*"

But the Writer didn't really need to picture it, for he'd already seen it with his own eyes. In Dawn's embalming suite, when she'd demonstrated her and Snowie's ploy to get sexual "action" out of the eight-foot-tall *dead* thing on the examination table. She'd merely pumped more embalming fluid into it, inflating it to whatever size she and Snowie desired. She'd pumped it up to something a little over a foot, and then she and Snowie traded off sitting on it, riding the Bighead's dead carcass like a horse until they'd each achieved shrieking, drooling, muscle-clenching orgasms.

At the very least, it had been a unique activity to watch, and it proved just how enterprising women could be...

And when the Writer had asked was it possible to pump the Bighead's cock–sorry, no other word will do–was it possible to pump the Bighead's cock up to even larger dimensions, both girls had cackled laughter.

Yes, it got *much* bigger, much bigger than any woman could stuff into her vaginal canal...

"I very much believe that the Bighead's genitals are incomprehensibly massive," the Writer agreed.

"And you've obviously heard aspects of the legend that say every woman the Bighead had ever raped–dies."

"Well, yes."

Charity rolled her eyes. "The cock on that monster is a killing machine. It tears a woman up, punctures her entire womb, hemorrhages everything. Men too. The Bighead was *horny all the time,* and when he couldn't find a woman to fuck, any man would do. Might as well hammer a log up his ass."

Charity's sudden use of sexual profanity the Writer found ambiguously erotic, and it didn't help for her to be lying there on that priceless couch with her toned, tanned legs stretched out, and the towel only covering her breasts from only a quarter-inch above the nipples. He didn't quite grind his teeth when he went on: "But you *did* survive. Was it just luck? Were you hospitalized for an extended period? Were you temporarily comatose?"

"No," she said, fiddling with a fingernail. "Nothing like that. You're not thinking the whole thing through."

His brow knit, but after a full minute he confessed, "I give up."

"The Bighead's my twin brother," she reiterated, seemingly gearing up for some manner of explication. "We're both hybrids," she began, "we're both part human and part something else–either demon or alien, according to the legends. That means we both have some human genes, and we both have genes from the something else, in varying amounts, some parts smaller, some parts greater. The Bighead's genitals are huge compared to a human's because of its genes, and he's also a monster because of those same genes. And since he and I both come from the same father, I possess some of those genes too, but I was lucky enough not to inherit the *monster* side of it."

The Writer's deductions slowly revolved around what she was saying, and it seemed, now, the conclusion was so simple, he was surprised it hadn't instantly occurred to him...

"But I did inherit some of his *other* genes..."

Of course, by then the Writer got it, just as you have.

Charity leaned up from the couch and turned to establish a proper sitting posture. "Remember," she repeated. "*You* asked." Then she fully opened the towel in order to expose her groin area, and spread her legs apart as far as they would go.

The Writer stared, his jaw dropped.

"Not very ladylike of me, I know," Charity said almost with a chuckle, as what she'd been intimating moments ago was now made plain to even the dimmest intelligence: the *other genes* that she'd inherited from her brother had been those governing *genital* development.

The Writer, still staring, thought to himself with virtually no conscious impetus: *That's the biggest pussy I've ever seen, even in underground comics! That's the biggest pussy I could ever imagine in my wildest nightmares! She's got a GIANT pussy! And I mean fuckin' GIANT!*

The designation of the word "giant" wasn't even close to describing the organ's overall effect once glimpsed. Glistening pink meat was of course the image's most salient feature, pink meat rimmed by a split field of dark pubic hair. Toward the top of this canyon-like gash showed a hooded bulb of similarly pink, shining flesh but in the shape of a hen's egg–clearly the clitoris. Lurking an inch below this was a rather puckered pink hole that the Writer suspected would accommodate his entire index finger–Charity's urethra, no doubt. And down the center of this, this, this *morass* of a vagina was a gap of about an inch wide but probably a foot long: the entrance to her vaginal canal, and exactly how deep this canal traversed, the Writer didn't care to contemplate, but of course it *had* to have been at least two feet in depth since the Bighead had once had its way with her and left her undamaged.

Charity herself, however, didn't seem the least bit awkward or concerned about showing her vagina (especially *this* vagina) to a man she didn't know. Quickly, then, she stood up and walked back and forth once. "See? When I'm standing you can't even tell 'cos most of it goes inward when my legs are closed." Then she sat back down. "And here's something else, I can make it a lot wider–watch."

The Writer continued to watch with his mouth hanging open.

Charity resumed her previous pose: legs parted nearly at a ninety-degree angle. Next, according to her face, she seemed to be exerting herself in some way, her eyes closed tight, her face darkening a bit, and then the cords of all her muscles began to stand out, and standing out, too–spectacularly–were the veins over most of her body, since almost no fat existed between her muscle and her skin. Added to this sight came the severe elucidation of that "six-pack" abdominal wall. Then–

Then–

That inch-wide gap down the middle of her vulva...began to expand.

Very slowly, yes, it widened, gradually opening to an aperture probably wide enough to admit a regulation football.

Then Charity relaxed, and the whole mess closed back up. The Writer didn't know when whether to throw up or applaud.

"So, there you have it," she said, much more cheerily than one might expect of a girl with a sex organ so anomalous. But then she seemed to catch herself: "Oh, damn, I'm sorry, I wasn't thinking. That must've grossed you out."

The Writer managed to choke out the most civil response he could, "No, no, not at all..."

"I've forgotten so much about modern society and people in general," she went on, and wrapped the towel back around herself. "I almost never even see *people* these days, except when I hike into town, and that's not often. I've forgotten how to act."

"Charity, there's plenty to be said about reclusion," he replied. "Some of the greatest philosophers have insisted that *other people* are the greatest impediment to one's self-actualization–"

"That sounds like Maslow and Sartre," she idly remarked.

The Writer was astounded. "You're right! How did you know that?"

"Oh, I went to college a long time ago–University of Maryland," she said, lounging again back on the couch, "and I took some Philosophy. It was fun but not very practical I guess."

"Indeed, an educational background in Philosophy won't pay many bills in the real world." He took another hit on his beer. "If you don't mind, please elaborate on what you implied earlier, that 'psychic vibe.' You mean a psychic connection to your twin brother?"

"Yeah, and a very strong one sometimes. I felt it twenty-some years ago just after I arrived in Luntville to visit my aunt. And then I started feeling it again very recently, and along with that vibe came some sort of an impulse–an impulse to come here, specifically, to this house."

This sounded very interesting. Psychic connections were regularly described by twins, as though coming from the same shared womb activated some sort of ethereal wifi between the two. "Why this house?" asked the Writer. "Any ideas?"

She shrugged. "I can only guess that it means something dire will happen here."

"Something that involves not just you, but the Bighead too?"

"Yeah. That's the feeling I have," she said. "I think the Bighead's coming here, because he knows *I'm* here."

Something unpleasant crackled in the Writer's head; all his muscles tensed. "If the Bighead's coming *here*, we should be heading as far away as possible, shouldn't we?"

"It's probably a good idea for you and the girls to leave, yes," she said in an offhanded way, "but then you'd be forced to abandon your friend downstairs. It's your decision. But me? I feel I *have* to stay here because it's kind of like my destiny."

And the Writer felt the same way, didn't he? That he'd returned to Luntville after all those years, even with very little memory of the place, because he was *destined* to. *My doppelganger said as much, and so did the old man Septimus Howard. I am The One...* But a more pertinent consideration came to mind at once. "So, then. You're staying here because you're sure it's your destiny. Have I got that right?"

"Yeah, that's pretty much it," she said.

"Is it because you believe that some kind of showdown will occur between you and the Bighead?"

"Especially that. It's because the Bighead and I *must* meet again."

"But if that happens, you'll get killed, won't you?" The Writer spoke the obvious. "The Bighead's an eight- or nine-foot-tall homicidal monster. In a confrontation like that, you can't possible expect to survive."

She looked at him with an aloof smile. "I might not, that's the chance I take. But then there's something you don't know."

The Writer's eyes seemed to double in size. "Please tell me!"

"I have a secret weapon," she said.

The Writer waited. He tapped his foot, looking at her and near cringing.

"I'll tell you about it when the time's right," she informed him next, and winked.

Just like a fuckin' woman, he thought, pursing his lips. *What did I expect?*

She crossed her ankles on the couch, stretching out, and didn't seem to care that one bare breast popped out from the towel. "But here's something I can tell you. Whatever you want to call that link that exists between me and my brother—intuition, psychic, precognition, whatever. I can tell you right this minute that the Bighead is very very close to us, and he's very very pissed."

* * * *

And this declaration of Charity's was very very true. The Bighead was very very close by and very very pissed off. Of course, it was the Bighead's nature to have a volatile attitude (he existed to rape and kill), and that female bear he'd sodomized–oh, and those two pregnant female prisoners he'd just taken care of–that was all just a matter of course. That was the Bighead being the Bighead. He'd popped those big, round, ridiculous bellies like soft gourds, and it doesn't need to be stated what he'd done with their contents. Those deeds were simply examples of his natural behavior, but now...

Now there was this.

This sudden and newfound rancor, the irritation that pecked at him like mockery–yes! Mockery!–like someone was making fun of him, like someone was laughing at him!

Nobody laughed at the Bighead.

He considered that perhaps it was just a side-effect of his brain growing back since he'd been so mysteriously brought back to life. He figured that at least a third of his "gray-matter" had been blown out of his skull all those years ago by that cocky priest with the big gun (and it had been a very lucky shot, since most bullets scarcely affected the Bighead). But now the brain was growing back and perhaps with the rigors of such regeneration came a few unfamiliar sensations, like this itching *buzz* he'd been carrying ceaselessly in his head now for several hours. It was more than annoying; it was like birds pecking at him but he had no way to kill the birds because they were in his skull. And, just as Bighead's damaged brain was quickly repairing itself, his memory was returning with more and more lucidity, and so was his intelligence. However, he had no idea what *portent* meant; therefore it would be impossible for him to make the deduction that these new aggravating sensations were premonitory. But–

Oh! there I go again! Bogging the reader down with a gush of unnecessary verbiage! I must cut to the chase, as I believe the saying goes, and reveal to you that the actual source of the Bighead's ire and irritation was this and only this: the smell of *pussy.*

Now, the Bighead *loved* the smell of pussy, the dirtier the better. But *this* was different somehow. It was *this* musky aroma that was mocking him. The smell wafted into his face like a steady sea breeze. Yes, this smell conjured him along like when you were in vicinity to a good barbeque place (only this wasn't smoked ribs and brisket, remember; this was *pussy!*) Worse was the sound that seemed to chaperone the aroma–just a drift of a sound at first, like 18-wheelers on an interstate miles away–and that was the unmistakable sound of female laughter, shouts, and also whistles. Finally, the Bighead stopped on the top of a hill and looked down. What he saw locked him in place. His single baseball-sized eyeball stared unblinking:

At the bottom of the hill he espied the large rectangle of land surrounded by the ten-foot-high chain-link fence which has already been described, and within that rectangle the dozens and dozens of teenage girls running back and forth kicking soccer balls (not that the Bighead knew what soccer was). Here was the taproot–indeed, the very *wellspring*–of the Bighead's itching agitation: the pussy-smell from all those pretty girls down there runnin' around.

By now the average reader needn't be told that the Bighead's senses were super-sensitive. His vision was like an eagle's, and his hearing like a bat's. Ah, but his *most* sensitive sense was his sense of *smell*. Like a hundred bloodhound-noses distilled down to one, the Bighead could smell the things he most craved from miles away–that's right. *Miles*. And now here he stood, not miles but just yards from a smorgasbord of pussy-aroma. It was an All You Can Sniff Buffet. Yes, sir, all those trim, young, athletic girl-legs out there running, and with each stride, puffs of delectable pussy-aroma gusted out of their little white shorts. Even mere *molecules* of the scent was pushed right through the fabric of those panties and shorts, and you can bet that Bighead's preternatural olfactory capabilities picked that shit right up, same way the snoot of a pit-bull picks up the distant scent of the Murray's Steak truck. And to the Bighead? Every single one of those pumping, sweating little pussies down there was a veritable raw porterhouse!

Okay. I see I've yet again belabored another not-terribly-important point. We understand just what it was that incensed the Bighead into a fever-pitch mental state, and no more need be said of such a feminine bouquet. All those girls down there and all their accommodating reverie had lit the Bighead's fuse. And now he was going to go down there and *fuck them all up* in a way that would be the stuff of legends...

* * * *

It was with nothing less than consummate virtuosity that Jimmy Limp Dick and his driver Zingo cut off the face of that female federal judge. Jimmy wielded the Bard-Parker #23 scalpel with a skill comparable to a plastic surgeon's (you can believe that he'd had *much* practice) while Zingo carefully lifted up the skin as it was methodically separated from the unfortunate woman's skull. Quite the bloody spectacle followed, and a noisy one. See, she was not quite dead, even after several serious Italian goombah beatings, ear removal, finger-and toenail removal, and being vigorously raped and sodomized at least twenty times. But you can bet she piped up fast once that pretty face started to come off.

Upon arrival at Luntville's Winter-Damon Funeral Parlor (you'll remember this to be Dawn's regular place of employment), the judge had been very securely strapped down to a stainless steel table back in one of the work-up rooms, her neck and forehead banded down so tightly that moving her head in reaction to this atrocity proved all but impossible. Augie manned the handheld so not to miss a moment of the diabolical payback; nor was a single note of the judge's screams missed by the quality Rode microphone plugged into the camera. And to describe the uniqueness of these screams pretty much defied the skills of the most deft writer. I can only suggest this: try to imagine what *your* scream might sound like, if *your* face was being cut off.

Nor was there any practicality in describing the judge's convulsions on the table as the deed was being done. Like slow electrocution? Like being blow-torched, or like having a big eyedropper full of hydrochloric acid shot down your pee-hole? No, none of that sufficed. No simile quite fit the bill.

At last, the limp "mask" of skin that had been the woman's face was fully removed. Paulie's eyes delighted at the sight: "Aw, shit, Jimmy! That's a piece of work if I ever saw one!" and then

Paulie, as sort of an adjunct to this remark, gave his crotch a penetrating squeeze. "Ain't that right, Augie?"

"Sure is, boss," Augie replied, now trying various camera angles to add a little creative pep to his film-work. Yes, sir! A regular Stanley Kubrick he was getting to be! A regular Ingmar Bergman!

But Paulie had already grabbed the mirror, for in instances as exciting as this, he was always thinking. "Don't die yet, Little Miss Judge!" he announced. The mirror was one of those oval kinds, with a handle, like women use. And certainly, the judge was not long for this world, but in these final ministrations, her still-awesome bare tits rose and fell such to indicate a respiratory rate of probably 200.

"Here's your last sight in life, cooze. See what that Harvard education got ya?" and then Paulie held the mirror over the area of space that was once occupied by her face. He wanted to make sure she could see it, and see it she did. Her eyes stared upward into the mirror for, now, nothing remained to close over them.

"How do you like me now, bitch?" Paulie chortled. "This is what happens when you give my name to the fuckin' newspapers! And you can bet, we'll send this video to your fuckin' husband, your parents and your kids. Hell, we'll even send it to fuckin' Harvard! And after that we put in on the Dark Web and make a shitload of money! Thanks, Your Honor!"

At that, all the men in the room broke out into hearty laughter; indeed, a fun time was had by all (well, all but the judge, of course). A few moments later, a death-rattle certified her departure from the realm of the living.

"*Damn*, that was fun!" Paulie went on, rubbing his hands together. "Shit, Jimmy, how'd you learn to cut off a face so good?"

Jimmy lit a cigarette and tapped the first ash into the judge's lipless mouth. "From your dear departed father, Paulie Vinchetti, Jr.–God rest his soul." He made the sign of the

Cross. "He showed me the right way, and come to think of it, it was, you know, back in the '80s. See, the Jersey City Police Commissioner nabbed one of his buttons and got him convicted of about twenty RICCO's and a bunch of Murder Ones, and Paulie, Jr., well, he didn't like that shit one bit. So he ordered me to snatch one of his kids but, see, the commish only *had* one kid, and it was, like, a six-month-old baby girl, so me and a crew bust into his house one night while the commissioner and his wife are at a fuckin' cocktail party at the mayor's. We raped the holy hell out of the poor baby-sitter and then did a necktie on her, then we make off with the baby..."

It would be a gross exercise of "superfluity" to go on with Jimmy's description of what we all know next took place. We don't really want to hear that, do we? But it will suffice to convey that by the recital's terminus, the mood in the rest of the room had gone down several notches, and Paulie and Augie's faces had both significantly lengthened and paled. However, Jimmy livened things up when he concluded, "But, guess what? That commissioner *never fucked with us again!*" and the room boomed with hee-hawing donkey-like laughter.

But now let's get back to the story in a more responsible fashion. Next, the peninsular-jawed Augie put forth a pertinent question: "So what do we do with the stiff, boss? Put her in the crematory?"

Paulie objected immediately, "Fuck no, not yet! We got more mileage to put on the bitch!" As Paulie said this, his hands were kneading the judge's breasts which, even now in her deceased state, were quite exemplary. "In fact, horny as I am right now, get that camera rollin' again, Aug. I'm gonna have to put some Sicilian gravy on these Wasp potatoes!"

So much for getting back to the story in a more responsible fashion. Augie filmed the spectacle, ever careful *not* to record his boss's face, while his boss, stepped up on a step stool, dropped his pants, unloosed his meager erection over the judge's dead breasts, and began to masturbate. Now, masturbating on a dead woman's tits seemed rather blase, and had been done a million times in novels like this, but you must understand that Paulie Vinchettii III was capable of a little creative diversity of his own and was well aware of its importance when producing "snuff-porn."

What he did, see, in a nutshell, was this:

He didn't masturbate with his hand, per se, he masturbated with the inside of the judge's severed face. This seemed a unique implementation of depravity, and provided—certainly (or at least *hopefully*)—a visual twist that customers of such stuff had never before seen. In moments, Paulie ejaculated mightily and shot a good four-inch spurt of "nut" across the dead woman's left breast. Not bad for a man in his late-fifties. Huffing and proverbially puffing, Paulie wobbled on the stool after the seminal delivery; in fact, Zingo rushed around to see to it that his employer didn't fall over.

Augie lowered the camera and gave a thumbs up. "Dead solid perfect, boss. *Great* money shot. Customers'll love it!"

Paulie smiled, regaining his breath. "So will the cunt's hubbie. Can't wait for him to see me jerkin' off with his wife's *face!*"

And, again, the room boomed with hee-hawing, donkey-like laughter.

Here a weary sigh from the author.

"The crematory now, boss?" Augie asked.

"No, no, not yet. Hold your horses." Now Paulie was eyeballing the dead judge's completely shaved or perhaps even electrolosized public region, along with the vulva, labia, etc. Even after a grueling number of Italian-thug rapes, that little gash and clit looked as cute as ever. "I mean, *look* at that pussy, will ya? It still looks good enough to eat, and we need to get some footage of that, right?"

Augie's mouth fell open in a way that seemed...*dreadful,* and then he, Jimmy, and Zingo all traded just as dreadful glances.

"Uh, uh, well, ya know, boss. There been a whole lotta dicks poundin' that shit, and a whole lotta cum pumped into it..."

Paulie didn't quite understand this interjection. "Yeah? So the fuck what?"

"Well, ya know, boss, we do anything ya ask but, but–"

Paulie cracked out a laugh. "Shit, Augie, I didn't mean for *you guys* ta eat her pussy! I mean, the chicks! The one-legger and Snow White!"

The other three men all relaxed in unison, and laughed. "Aw, yeah, a'course, that's a great idea, boss. But speakin' of those two redneck dim-wits, I haven't heard back from 'em yet. Left several messages. Seems funny. They always pick right up."

This information was not received with any positivity and at once seemed to threaten the Mafia boss's high spirits. Paulie's eyes narrowed. "Augie, please tell me those two cans'a tuna fish ain't *duckin'* our calls."

"Well, boss, I don't think so–er, at least they never did before, and they both know it wouldn't be good for their health if they did. I mean, you know chicks, boss. They're all air-heads, they're so busy yackin' and fussin' with their nails, they forget to charge the phone batteries."

Paulie crossed his arms. "I don't know, Aug. Way I see it, that shit ain't good enough. We give those two dizzy crackers a good deal, and we even *pay* em, and all they gotta do fuck dead guys with their dicks pumped up from the embalmer, eat a little corpse pussy for the camera, and mamby-pamby stuff like that. And this is the thanks we get, huh? Guess they think they're prima donners, must be too *busy* today to pick up their fuckin' phones when we call. They're probably grindin' their gashes together right now and *laughin'* every time the phone rings."

Augie believed this was an overreaction and, hence, too severe a condemnation, but of course he didn't dare put the idea forth verbally.

Now Paulie had gotten so worked up that his face darkened

and he was traversing his fist into an open palm. "And what makes it worse is–shit?–didn't we use one of our phantom companies to *pay* for their damn phones?"

"Sure did, boss," Augie said. "*Smart* phones, too, they was–expensive stuff, plus we pay their monthly service."

Paulie grinned, grinding his teeth. "Fuckin' bitches, I'll tell ya, huh? The more a guy does for a broad the more she treats him like he ain't there, like he ain't worth a pinch'a pig shit."

"I'll try the gimp again, boss." Augie started dialing. "Let her know we ain't foolin' around here."

"You do that, Aug. 'Cos I'm not likin' the things I'm thinkin' right now. It's gettin' my shorts in a bunch."

Tense, unpleasant moments ticked by as Augie got through to Dawn's voice mail. "Listen and listen good. You know who this is. I've left a fuckload'a messages and you ain't answered none of 'em. We're at your place right now and there's work ta be done, and you and the albino need to be here to do it. The boss thinks you're givin' him the brush-off and, well, *nobody* gives the boss the brush off. I'm gonna hang up now, and give you five minutes ta be callin' me back and sayin' you and Snow White are on your way here. And if you *don't*–" Augie whistled. "Mama, mia! It makes even *me* sick ta think that we're gonna do to ya's when we find ya," and then he hung up.

The room stood in silence; Paulie and his poker face paced back and forth in his Christian Louboutin shoes which annoyingly *tap, tap, tapped* on the cement floor, and as he did this, his eyes did not come off his watch. After the expenditure of five minutes, the *tapping* stopped, he looked at Augie, and said very calmly, "Augie? What is wrong with people? Do I have a dick on my face or somethin'? Is there somethin' about me that says SHIT HERE?"

"Naw, boss, it ain't you. It's them." Augie reasoned that it would be wise to support Paulie's paranoia, even though he knew that Dawn and Snowie had probably just turned their phone volumes down. "It's the chicks, ain't takin' us serious no more. It's a woman's nature to treat men like chumps."

Paulie's chuckle was as black as the bottom of the deepest mineshaft on Earth. "Yeah, well this is one chump that's gonna make those two cum-garglers *wish* they were that no-face judge on the slab."

"Sounds like a party, boss. We could do torso-jobs on 'em, then bring in the pits to fuck 'em and eat 'em. Would make for great footage, ya know? Or—shit—we could stuff 'em both in the crematory alive and just turn it on an off till they're toast. Or barrel-job the both of 'em while they're watching each other, or maybe—"

"Them's all great ideas, Aug," Paulie said, frustrated. "But we can't even play paddycakes with 'em till we fuckin' *find* 'em."

Augie nodded, then suddenly his countenance took on an appearance of deep concentration. "Wait a minute, boss. I think there *is* a way ta find 'em, now that I think of it. Lemme call Andy Ball And A Half."

"Our tech guy?"

Augie's *big* face accommodated a *big* smile. "Yeah, boss. See, I remember one time him tellin' me how there's a real easy way to *track* these smart phones."

"Track?"

"Yeah. We bought 'em through one'a our fake companies so that means we own the phones and accounts even though the bitches are the one's who use the phones. There's this GPS thing, or GSP, or whatever the fuck it is. Ya turn it on and it'll tell ya *exactly where the phone is*, even if the phone's turned off."

Paulie's mouth fell open. "You shittin' me, Augie? That's pure genius!" Paulie *cracked* his hands together he was so excited. (Truth be told, he even squeezed his crotch—*that's* how excited he was now.) "Oh, yeah, make that call now! I can't *wait* to get my hands on those two floozies!"

* * * *

A pleasant quietude claimed the Crafter house as the afternoon drew on. Charity had fallen asleep on the antique settee, which was no wonder considering the number of miles she'd walked in the past few days. Dawn and Snowie, of course, were still engaged upon their mission to buy a drone. And the Writer was enjoying a few moments to himself out on the porch, sipping his beer and contemplating the inscrutability of the sky.

It was far too placid a day to believe that there was an open door to Hell in the basement right now.

But then the distraction invaded him. *It's also hard to believe that the Bighead's biological twin sister,* thought the Writer, *is just inside lying on the couch...and she's got a vagina big enough to stuff a two-liter bottle of Diet Coke in...*

He couldn't imagine why such things were happening to him, nor why his life had become *this*. This pilgrimage to inconceivability, occultism, ghosts, doppelgangers, Lovecraft's unknown relatives, and a gallivant with a pair of awesomely breasted redneck nymphomaniacs in what *had* to be the most fucked-up town in the world.

But what am I complaining about? I'm a writer, and good writers always pursue new and unusual experiences with un-commonplace people, to make their writing intriguing and important. Like Hemingway, like Faulkner, like Stephen Crane who went across the world to fight in a war so his writing would be honest, accurate, and useful to the reader.

Or maybe, just maybe, all of this was just a bunch of arrogant literary bullshit.

The Writer shrugged. But speaking of writing, he reminded himself that he'd just gotten a three-million-dollar deal for his next book, a third of which had already been paid. Odder still, the book was complete back in his hotel room but he himself had only written one page. *My fuckin' doppelganger wrote the rest of it,* he recalled amid much aggravation, and he didn't like somebody else monkeying with his art. *Once all this Bighead stuff is over with, I need to read my own book. Then I'll have to send it in to my editor...*

At that precise moment, his phone rang. He expected it to be Dawn or Snowie with some information about the drone–which one to buy, perhaps, or perhaps to make some "chick excuse" as to why they're running late–but, no!

The caller was none other than the very man he'd just been thinking of: his editor!

"Why, hello, Mr.–" the Writer said.

"Hi, Mr. ___, it's me, ___ at Scribner's. How are you today?"

"I'm great," he said, more formality than truth. "What can I do for you?"

His editor laughed. "You're quite the comedian, sir! Of course I received the manuscript in this morning's mail and, of course, I read it immediately."

The Writer's brow knit suspiciously. "Oh, did you now?"

"Yes, sir, and needless to say, I'm blown away. It's exponentially better than even my highest hopes. The execs are all reading it now, and they're all practically on the floor as well." A chuckle. "You really pulled a fast one, sir! I had no idea the book had been finished all along."

Neither did I...

"At any rate, sir, I don't mean to consume your valuable time. I just wanted to let you know that the book is officially accepted, and a press release goes out in the morning. We'll be fast-tracking the production, of course; the book'll be out in three weeks."

All the Writer could utter in response was, "Uh, wow. That soon, huh?"

"Yes, sir!" the editor enthused. "You'll have complete cover control, naturally. I'll have samples to you in a few days. And last but not least, I've just wired the second part of your advance to your bank account–"

The Writer's phone dinged, this time with an email: THIS IS A BANK OF AMERICA WIRE TRANSFER NOTICE. $1,000,000 HAS JUST BEEN WIRED TO YOUR SAVINGS ACCOUNT. THANK YOU FOR BEING A VALUED BoA CUSTOMER.

Fuck, the Writer thought. *I'm an anti-materialist and I just got ANOTHER million dollars for a book I didn't write! Some young smart-ass who LOOKS like me wrote the fuckin' book!*

"Before I go, sir," the editor added, "let me just say that in my opinion your book is the most important novel I've ever read. It makes *The Grapes of Wrath* look like the scribblings of a idealistic student-hack. Have a good day, sir. I'll be in touch."

And then the call ended. *Wow,* came the flattest thought. *I'm better than Steinbeck...*

He thought it might be a good idea to call the girls and see how they were doing at the mall but, wouldn't you know it? The phone rang again at that same instant.

The screen read UNKNOWN NUMBER.

Great... The Writer knew full well who it was. He answered and said, "How the hell did you get the book to my editor?"

"You were too busy playing footsie with those two tramps," his doppelganger replied. "I simply put the manuscript in a box and overnighted it."

"Did you make a copy, at least?"

"No, why?"

"I haven't even read it yet! It's ridiculous! Now I have to wait till it's released to read my own book–"

The doppelganger cleared his throat. "*Our* book, if you don't mind. But it's more mine than yours. If I'd left it up to you, it *never* would've gotten written. And trust me, I did a much better job than you could've. That Steinbeck remark was meant for me, not you."

The Writer wanted to hurl the phone into the yard. "This is fuckin' MADNESS! You can't be real!"

"That's what Macbeth though about the dagger, too, right? The minute before he stuck it in King Duncan?"

"Shut up!"

"Listen, hubcap. I mailed in the manuscript as a precaution. Just in case."

"Just in case of *what?*"

Was there the faintest chuckle? "In case you don't make it." The Writer stared as he held the phone to his ear. "You mean...in case I *die?*"

"That's right, slim. In case you die. There's a whole lot of serious shit coming your way. But I've already told you that."

The Writer didn't appreciate the "hubcap" and the "slim" reference. "But wait a minute. It's pretty clear that you can see the future. So you should already know if I die or don't."

"Well, I don't exactly know *everything*–" Another chuckle. "Just *more* than you. You better get with it, Humpty. Instead of standing around, chugging beer, gaining more weight, and lusting after those two Ellie Mays–"

The Writer *had* to interrupt. "I don't drink *that* much beer–"

"Don't make me laugh. You drink more beer than Charles Bukowski, only *he* wasn't fat."

"I'm not that fat!"

Now his doppelganger was laughing outright. "Look in the mirror! Pretty soon you'll have tits like Snowie and Dawn combined! Beer piles on the flab, brother, especially when you're a senior citizen."

"I'm *not* a senior citizen!" the Writer bellowed but then a thought peeped in his head: *Well, not quite.* And when he bellowed, his man-tits bobbed. "Fuck..."

"Yeah. Fuck is right. Now listen up. There's not much time left, and you've got a lot to do. You hear those sirens?"

The Writer lowered his phone and listened, then he listened some more. "No."

"Well, you will. Right now, the Bighead is tearing the shit

out of a bunch of high school soccer teams. You know the old cliche about how French people make wine? They put a bunch of grapes in a big tub and then they squash the grapes by stomping on them? Well, that's what the Bighead is doing *right now*, only the grapes are teenage girls, dozens of them."

The Writer frowned. "What are you *talking* about? Soccer teams? Grapes?"

"It's because the Bighead is riled up, see? He knows something's not right, see–call it a wild hair up his ass. And it's all because of Charity, see? They're telepathically connected, and he senses that she's nearby, see? The Bighead knows that Charity–his twin sister–has the power to kill him, see?"

"Don't say *see* anymore!" the Writer yelled.

"So keep on your toes...if that's possible. I can only inform you of certain things, I *can't* manipulate your future. Shit, man. I don't want you to get killed. If you got killed I wouldn't be able to drink on your credit card anymore."

The Writer nodded. "I'm touched that you care so much about me. And how'd you get one of my credit cards?"

"Never you mind. But here's one thing I need to tell you. Don't let yourself get distracted by Charity."

The Writer frowned. "Charity?"

"Yeah. She's got the hots for you, wants you to do her."

The Writer *had* to laugh. "If I had sex with her, it would be like throwing a Slim Jim into the Mariana Trench. I mean, have you *seen* the pussy on her?"

"Forget about her pussy," his doppelganger advised. "Ever heard of situational deduction? What's the most *important question* you should be asking yourself about Charity? If you guess, I'll tell you."

Finally came a surge of intrigue and excitement. "She said she had a *secret weapon*. What is it?"

"That's not the right question, you cement-head!" the doppelganger yelled. "We went to Harvard *and* Yale, remember?

You should be *much* smarter than this! Aren't you curious about her heredity?"

The Writer peered into the sky, thinking. "Well, sure. And I asked her that but she doesn't know for sure herself."

"Oh, I think she's got a pretty good idea."

"What then?" The Writer was getting miffed, and where the *hell* were Dawn and Snowie with the drone and, especially, the beer? "All she knows is what the legend says. That the Bighead is a hybrid. One legend says he's part-human and part-demon, the other says he's part-human and part-alien. And if the Bighead's a hybrid, then so is Charity, because they're twins."

"Now we're getting somewhere...almost. Jeez, you're dense!"

"For dick's sake!" the Writer yelled. "What?"

"Put your thinking cap on a little tighter. You'll figure it out."

"This is all rigmarole! Tell me something useful! Tell me what Charity's secret weapon is, you snide pain in the ass!"

A long paused followed, then the doppelganger said, "You *really* want to know, don't you?"

"Yes!"

"Isn't it more interesting if you find out in due time?"

"No!"

"Hmm. Well, all right. I guess I'll tell you."

"Great!"

"Are you ready?"

"Yes!" the Writer wailed.

"Okay. Here comes your answer. Are you listening?"

"Yessss!"

The doppelganger whispered, "Charity's secret weapon is–" And then he laughed.

click

The doppelganger hung up.

The Writer's face reddened; he almost threw the phone. "That motherfuckin' PIECE of cock-sucking SHIT!" he bellowed.

Birds cawed and shot out of trees; squirrels and bunnies dashed away at the shock. It was interesting, at least, the way the vocal blast echoed all about the property.

The aftermath of the outburst wilted him in place. All he could do was lean against the porch rail and try to dispel this vague, annoying depression.

A sudden sound manifested itself: the sound of several persons running, and when he turned, he did indeed see two people—actually, two teenage girls—running across the front yard. Both wore identical apparel: white sneakers, knee-high white socks, white shorts, and white tunics, each with a black number on the back. They seemed to be running in a blind panic, with washed out looks on their faces, as if both had been exposed to some nameless horror which left them in a mute shock.

"Hey! You girls!" he called. "Are you all right? Do you need help?"

But neither girl replied; they didn't even seem to hear him and instead just kept running across the yard, then down the other side of the hill until they disappeared.

Strange, thought the Writer. *Teenage girls in what appeared to be white uniforms of some kind, like sports uniforms...*

Soccer uniforms?

Hadn't his doppelganger said: *Right now, the Bighead is tearing the shit out of a bunch of high school soccer teams...*

Perplexed, the Writer stared back into the direction whence came the two girls, and then he heard another sound, a sound rather distant, perhaps several miles.

Sirens, as of police cars and emergency vehicles. Lots of them.

* * * *

"Gawd dang, girl," Snowie chuckled as she walked alongside Dawn down the sidewalk of the cheery strip mall. Snowie's remark had been made whilst gazing at Dawn's backside, which looked quite nice packed into those little blue jean cutoffs, and the big braless tits swaying back and forth in the green

Army t-shirt only amplified the image's effect. And, yes, they'd found the Radio Shack and managed to buy not one, but two quadcopter drones, because there'd been a two-for-one sale. Mission complete but, no, neither of them had bothered yet to check their cell phones; hence, neither were aware of the multiple messages–complete with death-threats–left by Augie in their voicemails, and with that information, we can let a little suspense build...

Dawn walked along rather stoically. "'Gawd dang, girl' *what?*" she inquired.

"You must be wearin' space pants 'cos your ass is fuckin' out'a this world, and your tits are about to make me go apeshit. And my tongue *needs* to be in the middle'a your junk, and I mean *right now!*"

"Not today," Dawn said dully. "Not in the mood."

"What?" Snowie exclaimed. "Aint never knowed you no ta be in the mood ta have your cooter et!"

"Eaten, not *et,*" Dawn corrected. "I'm just not up for it right now. I'm kind of depressed I guess."

Snowie put her arm around her, as a gesture of compassion but also because it afforded her a fine glance down the Army t-shirt to show that wondrous cleavage. "Ain't no reason ta be depressed! 'Tis a beautiful day, and the sun's a-shinin' and the world's a-turnin' and the birds, they'se a-chirpin'–"

"Save it, Snowie. Don't try to cheer me up. I don't like what's been going on."

Snowie nodded as if at a revelation. "Oh, yeah, ya mean what with the Bighead comin' back ta life an' walkin' out the funeral parlor, and them demons in that *wee-gee* board makin' us upchuck on each other, an' Pastor Tommy dead as dogshit, 'an a'course that door ta Hell wide open in the basement–"

Dawn winced. "No, no, Snowie! I don't care about that shit! I mean the Writer, and that fruitcake woman with the long hair."

"Oh, ya mean Charity?" Snowie said. "What about her? She seems nice."

"Gimme a break, she's nuttier than a Pay Day–if they still even *make* Pay Days, and let's face it. You and me both got the hots for the Writer–"

"Well a'course! That boring fat fuck is *rich!*"

"–and I don't like the idea of him being in the house alone with her. I'll bet she had his dick in her mouth two minutes after we left."

Snowie's eyes narrowed. Her expression said she did not like the stead of Dawn's suggestion. "She better not, 'nless she wants me ta bury her skinny ass in Crafter's grave."

"Let's just get back to the house..."

But Snowie stopped abruptly at the next storefront. "Ooo, look! A pet shop! Look at the fancy turtles! And–all the froggies!"

Indeed, the storefront window boasted several fish tanks and terrariums. One such tank housed several exotic lime-green turtles with very flat shells and pointed heads with red stripes down the neck; each spectacular creature was about the size of a dinner plate. More than several big bull frogs made their abode of another tank. At Snowie's juvenile excitement, Dawn just frowned and shook her head.

An Asian man, grinning out the window, reached into the turtle tank, removed one inmate, then–

Snowie screamed.

–slipped a long knife into the animal's side between the shell, pried off the shell, revealing the gory, moving innards. Immediately thereafter, an Asian woman grinned out the window similarly, grabbed a big fat bull frog, slapped it down on the cutting board and–

THUNK!

–expertly chopped its legs off with a bloody cleaver.

The legs quivered, while the other part of the poor frog

tried to crawl away from the horror.

Snowie wailed and wailed. "Did you see what them awful people did!?"

Dawn yanked Snowie aside and urged her away. "That's not a pet shop, you dickbrain, it's a fuckin' Korean restaurant..."

But some commotion seemed to be taking place a few stores down; Dawn pointed. "What's all the hubub here I wonder?"

FLAT-SCREEN PARADISE! read the sign over the window, a T.V. and electronics outlet.

Several passersby had stopped at the big window, all seeming to be in some state of curiosity or even alarm. Several big-screen T.V.s were displayed in the front window, and all of them were tuned into the same news channel; the audio for this channel was being piped outside via speakers in the awning. What Dawn and Snowie heard first was this:

"–is being described by witnesses as a *massacre* in broad daylight, and in the least likely of places," came a female newscaster voice-over, "and an *attack*, apparently by only a single perpetrator. Channel 6 News has learned that the gruesome onslaught against dozens of Peasley County high-school girls began only an hour ago, in a fenced practice field just off Governor's Bridge Road, eleven miles west of Luntville..."

"What the fuck," both girls muttered.

Plastic signs on this big front window celebrated UHD! 4K! 6K! 8K! WE GOT IT ALL! BLOWOUT FLAT PANEL SALE! Naturally the establishment's most impressive models were propped up there for anyone walking by to see, and on the biggest of them there was being broadcast right now another news program, with a banner up top: SPECIAL REPORT! THIS JUST IN! MASS-MURDER AT HIGH SCHOOL SOCCER PRACTICE!

What Dawn and Snowie saw were police vehicles with flashing lights, EMTs hustling injured and bloody young women on stretchers, and wider shots of the inside of an immense, fenced compound, which hosted a soccer field, but the field was littered with bloodied female figures in white shorts, sneakers, etc., some obviously dead, others convulsant as paramedics worked on them. Strategically blurred, some of the girls lay nude, as if their clothes had been deliberately torn off their bodies, while a number of others lay unmistakably dismembered, disemboweled, or beheaded. Quite a few adults–apparently the parents of the victims–stood around either in shock, or wailing, or blubbering. "Where's my daughter?" an insane-faced father cried. "What did that thing do with my daughter?"

Another banner scrolled across the screen: SENSITIVE VIEWERS ARE ADVISED NOT TO WATCH, and then Dawn and Snowie along with several persons standing with them all squealed at the next series of clips, strategic blurring be damned.

1. A shot of the fence's most distant corner where a pile of blood-drenched bodied lay askew. It looked as if they'd tried to crawl over each other as something devastating had forced them into the corner and torn them apart....

2. Squiggles of entrails stretched this way and that, peppered by other organs, a breast here, a face there, a complete scalp over there...

3. A particularly ghastly sight: a 40ish red-haired woman in what appeared to be nursing attire lay spread-eagled in the grass, white skirt and panties ripped off her body, and her legs so obscenely spread that her hips had clearly become dislocated. Her splayed pubic area showed an agape hole out of which intestines and other things had spilled. From her opened mouth, too, a mishmash of internal organs accumulated, as if *forced* up her esophagus and out her mouth by some incalculable internal pressure.

4. One girl, with very large breasts and whose top had been ripped off–

Well, we could go on and on here, but you get the idea...

The next clip detailed a different female newscaster, the one even dowdier-looking than the last. "No gunfire was reported, and multiple witnesses have attested that the single perpetrator–a very large naked man with a bald head–entered the compound, deliberately locking the gate behind him, to prevent any girls from escaping. Then he herded the girls into one corner, and the slaughter began–"

Blah, blah, blah. This is becoming a very boring writing device, yes? The writing instructors tell us we must *show* the reader, not *tell* the reader. So I'm attempting to *show* the reader what happened by snippets on a television newscast.

And it ain't working.

Therefore I've elected to plow through the rest of this quagmire by *telling* the reader what happened in a brief narrative block.

The "perpetrator" corralled as many girls as possible into one corner and then tore into them bare-handed, his arms roving about like a threshing machine. Imagine someone corralling a pack of chickens into a corner with a lawnmower. Similar thing here, only the Bighead was the lawnmower, and several dozen screaming, hysterical high school girls were the chickens. Chunks of flesh, heads, arms, legs, etc. were ejected this way and that. Ropes of intestines flew like New Year's streamers. One poor girl–a sophomore named Patricia Browne–even had her uterus *pulled out of her vagina* by the monster's giant hand and it was flung a good hundred yards over the fence–a Just For The Hell Of It kind of move–not just the uterus, however, but also the ovaries, fallopian tubes, the whole nine yards. A fair number of girls who first made it to the corner managed to save themselves by scaling the fence and running like holy ever-living *fuck,* but those less fortunate young ladies who tripped, stumbled, or for whatever reason found themselves on the ground as the Bighead arrived...well, their heads were promptly stomped on and popped.

"Shit!" Dawn exclaimed. "I've seen that place! It's an old county motor pool or something, and now they use it for practice fields. It's only a few miles from the Crafter house!"

"And we both know it *had* t'be the Bighead that done all that killin'!" Snowie fretted. "Which means the *Bighead* is only a few miles from the Crafter house!"

"Come on, we gotta get back there," Dawn stipulated. "Let's go!" and with that turned from the store, and they both trotted off to the El Camino...their tits bouncing magnificently beneath their t-shirts. Moments later, rubber was burning, and the blazing white hot rod shot out of the parking lot.

But back at the T.V. store, shoppers remained, transfixed with eyes wide on the gruesome newscast. Now a hayseedish-looking middle-aged man was being interviewed on location by yet another very drab-faced newswoman. A legend at the screen's bottom read RUD GOODER, COUNTY EMPLOYEE, and he was saying in a very shaky voice, "It were unbelievable, it was. This thing just up'n walk in here like it own the place, locked the chain so's no one could 'scape, and hightailed it straight fer the girls, it did, an' I swear the ground shook each time this thing's foot hit the grass. It tore inta them poor girls all pushed back in the corner, rippin' 'em up, it was like they wasn't nothin' but stuffed dolls. Steppin' on their heads and bustin' 'em like cantaloupes, 'er tromping down on their bellies which send their guts all a-spewin' out their mouths. Blasted thing even ripped off the shirts'a some of the gals—the, uh, bigger ones, ya know? and—you know—felt up on their bosoms, and even pulled a few off bare-hand'n then started, ya known...*mushin'* 'em, ya know, like one'a them—dang! What're them things called? Stress balls! Then there was one gal, *pretty* girl she was, and I think it might'a been Betty Crink, and this thing grab her and strip her bare from the waist down just like that, and-and...then it pick her up in its big meat-hook hands like it was holdin' a *ham sammich,* and then it popped her like a balloon, it did."

The cock-eyed newswoman held the mike closer: "What exactly do you mean, Mr. Gooder? What do you mean it 'popped her like a balloon'?"

"What I mean, missy, is this thing pick Betty Crink up, put its mouth right smack dab against her–uh, I mean, ya know, her girly part, and then it done *blew into her,* like a *balloon...* and then, good Gawd! Then she up'n *pop!* Organs'n insides and what not all flyin' every which way. Then it grab onto poor Debbie Hillman, grab her one-handed by her hair, and then it start wingin' the girl round'n round over its head like someone doing, like, a *slingshot,* and he was doing it with so much force that poor Debbie's shoes, shorts and panties fly *right off her body,* so's I guess that be what'cha might call *centriferkle* force or what have you, 'an finally it got ta be *so much force* that her poor head kind'a *detach* itself from her scalp and she go flyin' off'n up inta the trees–"

Mr. Gooder turned, wiped another tear, and pointed upward. The camera jostled, zoomed, and focused, and there, laying twisted and disjointed in a large tree was the bare-from-the-waist-down and scalpless body of a teenage girl, and evidently that same *centriferkle* force had continued to work on her as she flew to her resting place...for the most strategic blurring could not hide how several loops of intestines dangled from her vaginal lips like a funky, puffy garland.

Poor Debbie Hillman!

When the camera returned, the newswoman's face was much paler than before, but still she wielded her microphone and went on, "But Mr. Gooder, if I may. You've repeatedly referred this barbarous murderer as an *it* and a *thing.* Don't you really mean that perpetrator was a very large *man?*"

Rud Gooder emphasized each syllable with a jab of his finger, like multiple knife-strikes. "No-I-do-NOT, young miss! It ain't no *man,* 'cos ain't no men ever grow eight, nine feet, like about what this thing stood. And lemme ask *you,* hon. Have

you ever knowed a *man* with a"–the next word was bleeped
out–"a coupl'a blammed feet long? Huh? Hard as gnarled oak,
too, it was, bouncin' up'n down as it run, and the end of it big
as a beefsteak tomato but with a *hole* in it. You know any *men*
like that? Naw, this weren't no *man,* and you's can ask anyone
who see it. And lemme tell you somethin' *else!*"

Here, Mr. Gooder pointed his finger directly at the camera.
"Bunch'a folks are sayin' it were one'a them Bigfoot things like
what ya see on them T.V. shows, only a special kind that ain't
got no hair on it, but all's I can say to that is it's pure malarky!
See, I remember the stories from back when, and I can tell ya
this sure as pigs can"–the next word was also bleeped out. "This
ain't no Bigfoot. It's the Big*head!* The Bighead is *back!*"

* * * *

In expensive hiking boots, khaki shorts, and one of those
many-pocketed fishing shirts, Mr. Michael Ling might easily
have passed for a serious southern outdoors man instead of
the Left Coast city denizen that he really was. With the stylish
shaved head and deliberate five-o'clock shadow, discerning
intelligent eyes, and a prepossessing demeanor, he was, in all,
an imposingly handsome man, such that he was something
of a "chick magnet" at his office. And speaking of his office,
Ling worked for the acquisitions department of a *huge* movie
production company in Los Angeles.

So you may be wondering why a man such as this would
be wandering around in the wilderness of backwoods West
Virginia. The answer to that can be supplied in very few words.
Ling was scouting for locations for what would surely be a
blockbuster horror movie called... Well, never mind what it's
called; that hardly serves *this* story, eh? Nor is it serviceable to
mention that a third of the film had already been shot, but the
remaining financing had yet to be procured!

But forget all that. Ling was scouting locations in the wild.

A fair amount of research had landed him here, and not to his displeasure. This area was perfect for the sort of movie his company was contemplating, and Ling took many photos with his preposterously expensive Canon 5D. He felt certain his employers would love this area as a film location: it was different from the typical "backwoods" cliches we've seen so many times before. It was restive to look at while at the same time conducive to the notion that something wicked was out there watching but not quite glimpsable.

Perfect! Ling thought, snapping one pic after another. And–

Wait!

What's that?

He stood amid a hilly clearing, but deeper within the surrounding trees he could swear his eyes detected some shadowy, symmetrical bulk. *Is that a building?* he wondered. It couldn't be a rock formation, no. It had to be something man-made. Though it might not be the greatest idea for a Californian to meander far into an unknown West Virginia forest (Snakes? Ticks? Beasts of the wild?) he could not for another moment resist pacifying his curiosity, so into those woods he now tramped.

His conjectures did not go unrewarded...

Soon Mr. Ling stood at the rear of a large and clearly archaic edifice. This rear area existed on an incline, such that the brick-and-mortar walls showed, until that incline leveled to flat land atop which stood a large rectangular building. In other words. that brick-and-mortar abutment was a basement which was buried save for this conspicuous outcropping.

However, and even more conspicuously, a ragged *hole* existed in part of this abutment, and it gave the appearance of being forcibly formed some long time ago, by a sledgehammer, perhaps, or some other blunt tool.

Now, did Mr. Ling see fit to *enter* this hole? Mr. Ling did not, nor did he even turn the flash on his camera, thrust it within, and take a few snapshots. There was something about this hole that was...

Ominous.

For one, a vague *smell* seemed to float from the aperture, a smell most unpleasantly reminiscent of very bad human body odor. Also, he heard–or *thought* he heard–something like a *slithering* sound, or a *sliding* sound.

He reconciled that this latter observation was most likely the product of the power of suggestion. But that odor?

It was real, and he didn't care to discover its source.

Still, his curiosity remained vigorous, so he stalked up the incline away from this basement abutment until he reached ground level. He needed to see for himself exactly what manner of building this place was.

A fuckin' log cabin? he pondered, because its proper walls were indeed made of very stout logs, stripped and stained eons ago, and the gaps between each log were sealed with beige mortar like that kind between the basement bricks. Sheets of ivy climbed up a majority of these outer walls, and probably the roof too. But one thing was for sure: if this place were a log cabin, then it was a *huge* one, so huge as to be impractical, Ling reasoned. In all, the entire structure duped his California sensibilities.

"Well, fuck," he muttered aloud. "I might as well check the whole place. That's what they're paying me for."

His goal was to see the actual front of the building. A structure like this, so long abandoned–for clearly it was just that–would probably not have a locked front door–if any remaining front door at all, and Ling did want to get a few shots of the interior if possible.

At this precise point in his walk, he had no reason to imagine that he would not even *make* it to the front door...

Ling stopped when he heard a voice, a *female* voice:

-who's that?-

Then another:

-who's he?-

What the fuck? Ling spun around but observed no source for the two voices. Best idea would be to get out of there, right? But, no, Michael Ling did not do that. Those voices sounded so creepy, yet so fascinating at the same time. And they seemed to project an *aural side-effect* to Ling, which was, well, the darnedest thing.

A second after hearing those two creepy female voices, Ling...got wood.

Wow, this is weird. Then he took a few more steps forward (in his $600 NewChic-brand designer hiking books. Only in California!), stopped again, and heard the voices once more:

-hello?-

-hello!-

This time Ling nearly jumped out of those fancy-ass Left Coast designer hiking boots. He'd heard both voices loud and clear this time, and with a resonance that seemed downright bizarre. He staggered backwards, in fact, so unaccountable and baffling were these voices. Mr. Ling stood wobbly-kneed, and it struck him that these voices might not even have registered in his ears, which sounded–pun intended–absurd. That last "*-hello-*" seemed to have caused a throb in his head, a throb like a pressure. *This is fucked up, all right,* he thought at his articulate best. And that throb in his head beat right along with the throb in his pants–all utterly mystifying.

More mystifying was what happened next.

Two figures emerged from the woods–two *cloaked* figures, or I should say two cloaked *female* figures, and this would not have been an unusual sight had he been back in La-La Land where he came from. Los Angeles was stuffed to the gills with fucked up, wacked out chicks who dressed in Halloween shit when it wasn't Halloween. But he wasn't in Los Angeles, was he? No, he was standing in the bumfuck wilds of West

Virginia–not La La Land, *Redneck* Land.

"Um, hi," Ling greeted, but beyond that he didn't know what to say.

The two cloaked women looked back at him and smiled. Their hooded cloaks were shiny, like black plastic raincoats, which must be insufferably hot, but not a bead of sweat showed on either white forehead, and it was then that Ling noticed just *how* white those foreheads were, and their throats, and the skin showing in the V's of where their cloaks were pulled together. They wore high shiny black boots, which divulged only their bare white knees and maybe an inch of their thighs: also very, very white. These women were *more* than pale. The little bit of their skin that showed was as white as white could be, like the paper-white of a bright computer screen. Their eyes were covered by black sunglasses.

This was some wacky spectacle to behold in remote West Virginia woods!

They continued to look at him, smiling, while Ling could only look back at them in the most intense confusion. *Post-Neo Goths?* he wondered. *And it sure as shit ain't Halloween...* "Oh, I see," he conjectured, "You ladies must be attending some kind of festival or something, right? A Wicca Jamboree, or Solstice Fest? That sort of thing?"

Of course, such suggestions were plainly ridiculous. No solstice *or* equinox was close to taking place, nor was it even remotely likely that some kind of "festival" would ever be held here. But Mr. Ling felt desperate for something to say while the two shapely women just stood there, their heads cocked, smiling. And one detail, left unremarked upon until now, was this: both women sported the most garish high-gloss crimson lipstick. Ah, yes, and one *more* detail:

Around the lily-white throat of each woman hung a necklace from which depended an upside-down cross.

Whoa, thought Ling as he took a step back. Now what

could explain *this* incongruence? *Oh, sure! They must be fans of a Norwegian black metal band. Sure! In West Virginia...*

By this point there was only one thing left to do.

"Well, ladies," Ling said. "It's been wonderful meeting you but I'm afraid it's time for my pilates class, so I have to go now. 'Bye."

-wait!-

-don't go yet!-

Their response clanged in his head 'til his temples hurt, and this was when Ling realized full well that their voices *were* sounding in his head, and not through his ears. In fact, it was indubitable.

The women's mouths had not opened when they'd conveyed the words to his brain.

-we wish we could be you,- one of them said in a tone that seemed very sad.

The other's next remark came with more vigor: *-don't you at least want to kiss us?-*

At *that* question, Ling frowned. He did not want to kiss either of these women; they were too fucked up. Yet when one stepped forward, Ling found it impossible to back away, and like a dream or a mushroom hallucination, the image of the woman's face began to wobble and float closer, and then those awful, glossy-red lips parted and–

Another mental sound shocked him, something like the sound of when you release air from a full tire, something like: *psssssssssssssssssst!*

* * * *

Back at the Crafter house...

As you might well imagine, things were gearing up to a scenario where one thing, certainly, was going to lead to another. The sedate summer day was cooling off, the sun preparing to lower itself and its radiance into the realm of early twilight.

The abrading and almost electronic sound of countless locusts began to die out, to be slowly usurped by the much more pleasant chorus of crickets.

The Writer was getting bored, so he repaired back inside the house where Charity remained asleep on the preposterously expensive antique couch. One breast remained out over the big white bath towel that sufficed for a robe, and the Writer found it beyond his capability to look away. He was a decent, cultured, and civilized man—true—but just now he was in quite an intractable mood of angst; what I mean is such angst as the kind inspired by more primordial synaptic firings in the brain.

It was *quite* a breast—not that Dawn's and Snowie's weren't, but, alas, theirs were "old news" just at the moment. Instead, *Charity's* breast—oh, why mince words in this trashy novel? Charity's *tit* sat there in a state of organic succulence; it was so intriguing, its perfect size, its plumpness, its saglessness in spite of being nowhere near any manner a bra for twenty-some years. Additionally, its hue—that rich natural suntan—only ameliorated the overall libidinous quality of the image. The big brown erected nipple stuck out like it meant business, the papilla (is *that* what its called?) filled with excited blood, such that the Writer peered more closely and wondered if Charity's subconscious were reveling in thoughts of a lustful kind.

Thoughts of a lustful kind, too, swilled densely about the Writer's head. *Damn! What a great fuckin' tit. I could jerk off on it right now and leave a little present on that GORGEOUS nipple.* Yes, that's what he thought, all right, and what a luxury such an act would be, to just say *yes* to his Cave Man Desires and *bust a nut* all over that great big beautiful "chest melon..."

Then the Writer winced himself out of the muse, ashamed. *What the hell is wrong with me?* He was sexually exploiting an innocent woman in her sleep, reducing her to sexual parts, using her for mental toilet paper. It was sexual malfeasance, intransitive rape almost, and it wasn't like him one bit.

He turned away briskly, lips pursed. *Why don't those damn girls get back here so I can get my mind off shit like this?* He plodded about the front room, making busy work for himself, glancing at bookshelves, framed portraits probably worth a fortune, more opulent 18th Century furniture. He forced himself to think about something other than Charity's tit, like the traversion bridle wide open downstairs, pretty much a door to Hell. Or those two girls he'd just seen outside, running away from something–two girls in *soccer* uniforms, and his doppelganger had said something about the Bighead and female *soccer* teams, hadn't he? Why did the weird or even impossible phone conversation seem so vague now? Indeed, it seemed barely existent, such that he wondered if he'd had it at all.

Wouldn't it be great, he mused, *if my entire life and all this crazy shit happening...was just a hallucination?*

He moved to examine a tall Swedish armoire, evidently late 16th Century, hand-crafted from Acacia wood, with gold inlays suggesting foliage. In a warlock's house, of course, you never knew what you might discover when poking around in such ancient cabinets, so it was with some reserve that he opened one of the doors. But no occult trinkets were in wait, just–of all things–a big Sony television and a cable box. *Some antiquary,* the Writer thought with a smile. *A warlock with cable. I wonder if Crafter has Hulu...*

The Writer yelped and nearly–pardon the tired expression– jumped out of his skin, when a very unexpected hand reached around his hip from behind. Naturally, the hand caressed his crotch and, of course, it belonged to Charity.

"There you are," she whispered. "I didn't hear you come back in."

By the time the very startled Writer turned around, the woman's hand had slipped down the front of his pants and was harassing his penis to full erection. Now Charity was naked, her towel on the floor, and her big, tanned, pucker-nippled breasts–er, I mean *tits*–pressing against his chest.

Momentarily, his pants were open, his "junk" out, which junk she did grab most ardently, and then she began to pull him backwards, back toward the couch, whispering, "Come here, come here! Let me take care of this! It's been *so long* for me..." She continued back-stepping, yes, still pulling him by his genitals, and that's when this neat little observation occurred to him. *A guy's cock and balls function very effectively as a convenient carry-handle by which women drag men through life...*, but, mind you, he wasn't complaining.

The Writer quickly became an automaton in Charity's hands, a stooge, a meat puppet, very ready to do its master's bidding and incapable of independent thought. (Some women have this effect on men, in case you didn't know that...) Remember, Charity's hair–having not been cut in twenty or so years–hung nearly to the floor, so she had to reach behind her and move it aside. Then she plopped her butt right down on the couch, pulled the Writer forward, until a perfect position for fellatio was effected.

Charity looked up, wanton-eyed, grinned, and whispered quite lasciviously, "It's been *so long* since I've hard a cock in my mouth," and I'll only go so far as to say that this unduly extended period of abstinence ended right then and there. I'll spare you the lewd details, not so much out of a writer's discipline but simply because, at this point in my career, I *will not write* another blowjob scene; I just don't have it in me. I'd sooner do yardwork...and I don't *do* yardwork. Instead I'll truncate the matter and let you know that very little effort was needed to trigger the Writer's orgasm, and it was at the exact moment of this breaking point that Charity slipped her mouth off his tremoring erection, jerked it the rest of the way off on her big right breast. She wielded his penis much like a baker decorating a cake, even partially succeeding in "drawing" several circles around the breast, saving the last eddy of sperm to glaze that big, pert, erect nipple and shine it up in grand style. It all looked keenly akin to that sugar sauce they use for honey-dipped donuts...

Whatever moans, utterances, etc., that escaped the Writer's lips at this moment of crisis will go unmentioned, but it is true that his knees nearly gave out, leaving him with no choice but to flop down hard on the couch, huffing and puffing, pants still down, and genitals still displayed. Even his tongue stuck out in a ludicrous aftermath.

Charity nudged him–"Look, look!"–and then showed him what she was doing: rubbing the sperm all around that big, tanned tit, like some earthy organic lotion. Exhausted as he was, the Writer stared at the very pornographic image with some interest; it even occurred to him that just moments ago he'd fantasized about doing the exact same thing to her, though by this point, it was not a profound coincidence, was it? Lots of kooky stuff was going on, including psychic flashes, deja vu, and other such departures from what we might think of as the terrain of normality. (That terrain went out the window a long time ago.)

The Writer slumped where he sat, and leaned against Charity as he tried to recuperate. She leaned against him too, sort of snuggling, and with her left hand–*not* the same she'd rubbed around on her semen-slopped breast–she grasped the Writer's right thigh, squeezed, then slid it a bit higher. "Maybe now," she cooed, "you can do something for me..."

This happenstance locked the Writer up in mental rigor mortis. A dreadful glance to his genitals revealed only a pathetic sack with two lumps in it, and a little flesh-toned mushroom cap on top. *I'm SPENT,* he thought. *My dick is DEAD, and it's gonna be that way for a long time.* Yet, even in the most ideal conditions, the truth of the matter could not be escaped.

Now, I'm sure you haven't forgotten a conspicuous detail already noted: that due to Charity's divergent heredity, she was possessed of a HUGE vagina. The Writer took another fearful glance at it just now, as Charity leaned affectionately against him and let her legs part, and there it was, an unavoidable sight: a fucking HUGE vagina, rimmed with brown hair.

Huge, I say. *Colossal. Immense.*

The Writer had never seen a vagina on, say, a water buffalo or a hippopotamus but, shit, they *had* to be along the same lines in size. *Fuck,* the Writer thought. *I'd need a leg of lamb in my pants to bang her.* In fact, the cleft of the thing started at her anus and went almost all the way up to her navel; it could've been an overstuffed foot-long roast beef hoagie...but with hair around it.

And now the Writer's hyperactive sense of politeness and good manners completely collapsed.

What could any man say to a sexually pining woman whose vagina was too big to fornicate with? The best the Writer could do was this: "Um, well, Charity, believe me, nothing would please me more than to be able to bestow upon you the same proportionate pleasure that you just bestowed upon me, but..." He gestured to his hilariously limp penis. "...even if this were in the best working order, I'm afraid–I'm afraid, um–"

Charity laughed and slapped his thigh. "Oh of course I know you could never fuck me! My pussy's too big! No normal guy could *ever* fuck me." She slithered over closer to him and with surprising strength pulled him over and tongue-kissed him, then she whispered, "But I think we can work something out..."

* * * *

Now we must shift locations, and I beg your indulgence to ask you to remember from Part 2 that the most inventive of the sociopathic Larkins quadruplets was killed most spectacularly by the Bighead (imagine a one-gallon hot-water bottle pumped up with 50 gallons of beef stew until it explodes; *that's* pretty much what happened to Horace.) Upon the discovery of what was left of that exploded "hot-water bottle," the three remaining brothers flew into a rage, and when *these* boys flew into a rage, you could bet that trouble was coming down the pike. Clyde and Gut headed east, and Tucker headed west, all now embarked on a mission to find out who (or what) had so heinously murdered their brother, and to royally fuck that person (or thing) up once found.

And here they are, the two of them, marching determinedly up a scenic incline between two lofty forest belts. They were armed with machetes because they eagerly anticipated throwing a hacking party on Horace's murderer. Now, perhaps you'll recall that Gut was the "pea-brain" of the four brothers, and quite given to superstitious claptrap—for instance, it was not far removed from his perception of possibility that the *Bighead* was responsible for Horace's atrocious murder, while Clyde (like Tucker) possessed more realistic suspicions. Be that as it may, as both of these large men labored their bulk up the hill, Clyde winced with some considerable angst, and squeezed his crotch.

"Good gawd *dang,* Gut!" he complained. "I'se horny as *fuck,* I am! I'se so horny I could fuck me a handful'a salamanders. When we find the evil motherfucker who done kilt Horace, I'm a-gonna fuck him in the ass till he starts upchuckin' his own shit and chokes on it."

"Shore, Clyde, but you mean if it really is a *him* and not—"

Clyde gnashed his teeth in disapproval of his brother's dim-witted inference. "Put a lid on that crap, Gut. I don't wanna hear no more 'bout the Bighead. That ain't but a silly-ass superstition. Ain't no such thing as Bighead just like there ain't no such thing as the Easter Bunny—"

"But dang it, Clyde, I seed the Easter Bunny with my own eyes when I was a tyke! I done told ya all about it!"

Clyde sputtered to himself. "Aw, shee-it, Gut. That weren't the Easter Bunny, that was just Daddy dressed up in a bunny suit. Me 'n yer brothers never tolt ya on account we didn't think ya'd understand."

Gut's fat bulbous face bloomed with incredulity. "Wha-What'cha takin' 'bout? Daddy wore a *bunny* suit?"

"Well, yeah, I'se afraid so. I mean, we all know Daddy weren't the normalest guy in town, not like other kids' daddies. See, Daddy, he was in this sort'a club—"

"Ya-ya mean like a golf club?"

Clyde winced. "No, no, shit, Gut, not a fuckin' golf club. It was like a jeep club like what some fellas are in, bunch'a dudes who all own jeeps and like drivin' around together on weekends, or like-like a *chess* club where people who like to play the chess all get together'n do that. But, Daddy, see, he were in what they call a *furry* club, which is where folks hang out together who like wearin' holler-ween-type animal suits, and, see, Gut, a lotta these furry clubs are, well, you know, they'se *sexual,* and in Daddy's case it were *homo*sexual, and once ever month or so he'n his furry-club buddies would get together in their animal suits and, like— and, like— well, they'd fuck each other in their butts'n suck each other off. Ever-one was a different animal, see, like Henry Wheeler was Bullwinkle Moose, 'n Old Man Matthews was Yogi Bear, an' on an' on like that—bet there was fifteen fellas in Daddy's furry club—and Daddy, well, I mean Daddy, he always had a thing fer bunnies so he was Bugs Bunny, and it were always him to be the first to take it up the ass from all the other fellas. Shit, his bunny pants even had a special trap-door over his butt just ta make it easier fer him ta git butt-fucked." Clyde just shook his head and kind of chuckled. "One night me'n Tucker peeked in the livin' room when we was suppose to be asleep, and that's what we saw—Daddy's furry club."

Gut stared open-mouthed, speechless at this rather idiosyncratic revelation.

"So's, anyway," Clyde said, "that's that and there ain't no Easter Bunny just like there ain't no Bighead, so keep yer dumbass yap shut about it, and look down yonder." With this,

Clyde stopped a moment and pointed toward the upcoming forest. "That look like somethin' ta you, somethin' past them trees in the woods?"

Indeed it did. A darker and more symmetrical shape seemed to exist deeper in the midst of all those oaks and pines: a long rectangular-shape, something clearly man-made. Gut's big man-tits jutted out in an attitude of authority as he shielded his eyes and peered intently. "Danged if you ain't right, Clyde! Too big, I reckon, ta be a house but it shore does look like some kind'a buildin'... and—" He looked over at his brother in a churning confusion. "You sure Daddy were really a *furry?* I mean, you sure you ain't just makin' the shit up so's I wont believe in the Easter Bunny?"

"Shut up'n come on," Clyde replied, trying to forget the fact himself. Instead, he felt it imperative they discover what this shape in the woods could be, and it wasn't more than five minutes later that they were standing beside it, looking up.

Gut's speculation proved correct—it *was* a building, and a long one: nearly 100 feet by 50 feet. Its long side-walls were made of stout logs—oak, by their looks—that had been stripped of bark long ago, darkened by some archaic varnish, and whose seams had been filled in with some just-as-archaic form of cement. Many years had obviously passed between now and the last time this pace saw any use, for the outer walls were crawling with vines and ivy.

Gut scratched his buzz-cut head. "Big-ass log cabin..."

"Cain't be a cabin, Gut. It's too big. Must be some kind'a school built way back in olden times like when Columbo were discoverin' America."

The roof appeared to be made of tin, and not in the best repair, and several slat windows—all of much later date than the original structure—had been cut into the log-forged sides, but most stood bereft of glass.

The heavy booted footfalls of the two brothers crunched

loudly as they moved forward to investigate the front of the structure. "Well, would ya lookit that?" Clyde said, glancing high upward. Old fieldstone bricks composed the front wall of the edifice, which rose to a peak and was topped by a cupola and bell tower (but no bell.) Heavy wood slabs with iron hinges formed a great double-doored entrance, and a lancet-style window existed on each side of the stone-block door-frame, with lead inlays. Clearly, these had once served as stained-glass windows. Between these lancet frames, the double doors, and the bell tower, Clyde was first to speculate, "This place must'a been a *church* when it was built..."

Gut nodded. "But a dang *big* church. And look at that there..."

Gut's fat finger (a finger, I'll needlessly mention, that had probed many a backwoods "cooter" and had gouged out many trespasser and drug dealer eyeball) pointed to a keystone of a different hue at a low corner of the brick front. The stone had been inscribed by a skillful chisel LAUDEM DEO - WROXTON 1698.

Gut tried to pronounce, "Wuh-rocks-ton..."

A vague recognition tinted Clyde's eyes. "Aw, yeah, I 'member hearin' 'bout this place back when we was teenagers. Ain't a church but some kind'a Christian-type school or–no!–a *hospital* or some such, for religious folks. In fact...." Here, Clyde nodded slowly as he was able to remember a bit more. "That's right. This is the place where all them kooky stories say the Bighead got kilt, by a *priest,* 's'matter'a fact. T'was around back wheres there used ta be a lake that got drained. That's where they say the priest shot Bighead right in his little eye and it blowed all'a Bighead's brains out, and they say his brains was a *yellowy green.*"

Gut jumped up on tip-toes as his mouth opened to a great big O of exclamation, "Oh, so you *do* believe in the Bighead!"

"No, I don't, ya dumb-ass hog-shit fer brains idjit! Alls I'se said was it were part'a the legend. Now shut up'n come on!"

Gut's eyes thinned in the deepest thought, which wasn't very deep. "Well then what the fuck, Clyde? Why not we go 'round back'n look there first?" Gut chuckled. "'Nless you're scairt..."

Clyde kicked his brother in the ass so hard it made a sound like a heavyweight boxer gut-punching an opponent.

"Oww! What'cha do that fer?" Gut wailed.

"'Cos yer a dick-brain! And if'n ya wanna look in back first, fine! But *you* lead the way, brother!" Clyde grabbed Gut by his fat neck and guided him toward the rear of this very strange structure. They scuffed down the slight hill and were quickly standing at the rear of the building which abutted the incline and showed evidence of a basement made from crudely cut fieldstones some long time ago.

Once there, however, both were stilled and silenced. A hole had evidently been knocked into this wall of irregular fieldstones, leaving an entryway large enough for a man to walk through if stooping.

"Looks like someone busted a hole in the wall," Clyde said, "but a long time ago, on account'a the ivy'n shit."

Gut's lower lip trembled. "Buh-bet it were the Bighead. Bet he's in there now–"

WHAP!

"Oow!" Gut wailed again when his wiser brother gave him another kick in the rear.

"Shut yer hole 'bout the damned Bighead! We'se looking fer the scum what up'n kilt our dear brother Horace, and that hole looks like a damn fine hidin' place, so come on!"

Each man upraised his machete in an attitude of command, then took turns entering the hole (not easy for either brother, given their size and weight, and a bit of a task for Gut because he was the plumpest of the two). Inside, the only light was the daylight that came in through the hole, but this shock of darkness was not what they noticed foremost. In fact, Gut actually reeled where he stood at the sudden, none-too-pleasant odor of these confincs.

"Fuck, Clyde!" Gut gagged outright. "Place smell like a meth-whore's butt-crack, and I'se mean one that ain't warshed in years!"

"That it do, brother," Clyde agreed. He took in a big sniff and squeezed his crotch in a definite gesture of auto-eroticism. "And I *like* it! We gotta find out where it's comin' from."

"But we cain't barely see nothin' it's so dark," Gut complained, still appalled by the smell.

Clyde shook his head, taking the small flashlight out of his back pocket. "Then git'cher flashlight out, numbskull! I gotta tell you ever-thang?"

Wait a minute. Flashlights? Did I mention previously that the duo had equipped themselves with flashlights?

No, I see I did not.

But you can take my word for it. They also brought flashlights. So what if I didn't mention it before? It's *implied.*

The powerful flashlight beams plowed through the inky subterranean space, revealing some very old cardboard boxes full of rotting prayer books but, surprisingly, little else worth remarking upon. Except–

"The hail's that, Clyde?" Gut asked, holding his light still. "You see that?"

Clyde saw it, and he nodded, "it" being a pile or heap of something.

"Dangedest thing," Gut said, squinting. "Looks almost like a pile'a old clothes, don't it?"

"Shore does, Gut, but the thing is...a pile'a old clothes don't *move...*"

The pile had to be about 30 feet away, and it was, indeed, moving. It seemed to be quivering, sort of jello-like, but then how could something jello-like in any way resemble a pile of *old clothes?* And then?

The "pile" began making noises. And strange noises they were. They seemed human, or nearly human, bleating-like, perhaps, and–somehow–desperate. Additionally, these noises had different tones, almost like voices from different *people...*

"Bluh-blub-glarub-hey!"

"Glet buh-bluss glout!"

"Hellub-hellup us!"

"Fuck this shit, Clyde!" Gut exclaimed.

"Calm down, sissy britches. Whoever's making them funny noises is 'bout to get their asses kicked by us, and horny as I is right now? Fella or gal, I'll be a-fuckin' one of 'em. Even if they'se sheep!"

Both brothers slowly approached the "pile," which *was* moving, all right. Their flashlight beams blared down. First they detected a "slithering" sound, then more of the voice-like bleating.

"Glelp us, bluh-bluh-blease!"

"Wuh-lotch out!"

"Guh-larup! Glub glub glup!"

Clyde squinted. "The *fuck!* It's a *pile,* all right!"

"'Tis a pile of *people!*" Gut yelled with eyes bugged.

And that it was. A pile of people. Four or five of them, probably, and they were all nude with their old mostly handmade clothes strangely laying atop this quivering pile made up of their bodies, almost as if the wearers of the clothes had somehow *shimmied* out of them just via errant movement.

Now, the author doesn't seem to be making himself clear, correct? What the fuck is he talking about? A pile of nude people? Their clothes not on their bodies due to *errant movement?*

Sometimes being a writer is hard, and it's especially hard being an *old* writer. Those creative synapses don't fire quite as fast nor as abundantly as they used to. Yet, my obligation, dear reader, is to *you,* and I will tread through Hell and High Water to help your mind visually capture the conundrum which was now taking place in that dank and very stinky fieldstone basement.

Five people exactly comprised this human pile. And wouldn't you know it? All five were female, which might be construed as deliberately sexist, an overt gesture to exploit, subjugate, and degrade the female of the species, to depict them as unwilling sexual receptacles and lightning rods for outlandish, gratuitous abuse, and symbols of the wares of misogyny, something that *male* horror authors are perpetually lambasted for. Well let me tell you something: such accusations are pitiable excuses to legitimize critical attack. These construsions are, in truth, *mis*construsions (faulty construction and all!) and the reason that the five human components of this suspicious pile are female is because that's just how it is in the story!

Pardon the digression.

Imagine five naked creeker women (these gals were creekers, yes, hence the handmade clothes) all lying on top of each other in something like a pile. Now...further imagine that all five were somehow completely *boneless*.

That's right. *Boneless*. As if some horrific virus had *dissolved* their bones.

I mean, no skulls, no rib cages, no arm bones or leg bones, no hip bones, no feet bones, no nothing.

So what might this *pile* look like then? Perhaps something akin to what's being described here? At any rate, it is my sincere hope that you get the picture.

This closer proximity to the pile only condensed that awful ass-crack-and-B.O.-odor to an outright stench. Gut, in fact, was teary eyed at it, and still hacking and gagging. But Clyde just leaned over the pile, intrigued, not repelled. He reached down and dragged some of the squirming sacks off the pile, then held one up by a rubbery arm. "Yep, they'se people, awright. *Boneless* people, Gut."

"Buh-boneless?" Gut stammered, still dizzy in the stench.

Clyde nodded. "You bet'cha, brother." He shook the one he held aloft, and all it did was flap around like one of those inflatable love dolls but with no air in it. "And it's a gal, see? Got a pussy on it." He indicated the weird triangle of black hair where the two rubber legs joined, then fished around the morass of hair with an index finger until–"Yessir! There's the hole!" he celebrated. When he withdrew the finger and sniffed it, he stamped his boot, gagged, and cut loose an expert Rebel Yell which echoed all throughout the cavernous basement.

Gut wobbled wearily in place, a hand to his belly. "Aw, come on, Clyde. This place is all fucked up and the smell's killin' me, it is. This pile'a boneless folks is gonna make me have nightmares..."

"Aw, don't be such a baby." Clyde dropped that first girl (who *slapped* on the floor like a wet flesh-colored beach towel), then rummaged through the rest of the human pile. "How ya like that, Gut? They'se all of 'em gals! Guess one's as good as another ta fuck." He dragged one squirming girl-thing away from the pile by her blond hair, then arranged it into a starfish sort of fashion.

The arms and legs moved like slow snakes, and the face on the flat, skull-less head looked up aghast at Clyde. A slack mouth moved and a tongue lolled. More bleating noises came out: "Guh-helerelp me! Glive mlee black mur-eye blones!"

Unaffected by the poor girl's plight, Clyde "dropped trow." "I ain't got'cher bones, honey, but right *here's* a bone fer ya," and with this comment he flexed an erection that was anything but small.

"Ya shitting me, Clyde!" Gut objected in a near whine. "This place is fucked up! We gotta get out'a here! Ain't no time fer you ta git'cha a piece'a ass!"

But Clyde was having none of this. "Won't take but a minute fer me ta bang a load inta this skinbag's cooze. Just like Mr. Fitzwheeler teeched us way back in Sunday school, two things a fella can never waste is food'n pussy, on account of these is God-given blessings. Shee-IT, t'wud be a sin fer me ta *not* stick some meat up this boneless fuck-dummy's cooter."

Gut winced at this entire situation, and he sure didn't remember Mr. Fitzwheeler ever talking about *pussy* in Sunday school. Meanwhile, Clyde's big old ass bopped up and down on this flat-as-a-matt boneless girl with whom he somehow managed to effect coitus. And in another moment, "Ah-ah, there she blows!" Clyde grunted, having successfully transferred his sperm into the girl's flaccid sexual orifice. Her just as flaccid head wiggled at little, and the eyeballs slipped out of what once were sockets of bone, but no more.

Then the poor thing's throat released a wheezy sound like: "Guh, gluh, glaaaaaaaaaaaaaaah..."

Clyde nodded and said, "You're welcome!"

Gut scratched his head, looking the way one does when one is making a critical contemplation. "Hey, Clyde? What'd'ya think would happen if'n she got pregnant? Ya think the baby would be, like, a *boneless* baby?"

Clyde was flapping excess sperm off the end of his dick, some of which flew right into the girl's agape mouth. "Well, hail. Gut, that shore is a good question, but I don't know nothing 'bout this boneless business. Guess it's a disease that ya catch from, like, a skeeter er somethin', which give ya a germ that, like, makes yer bones melt, like this one I heard 'bout that melts all your insides'n turns 'em into, like, soup, so's then ya shit it all out and croak. And now there's this other one startin' ta show up 'round these parts called Lime Disease. Ya can get it from a infectered tick, and what it does is, it turns ya into a great big lime with arms'n legs, and that's how you gotta spend the rest're life. A great big *lime* walkin' 'round! Guess there might be a Lemon Disease too, and Orange, Grapefruit—who knows?"

This situation was getting to be more than Gut's pea brain could cope with. It was bad enough to discover, after all these years, that his long-deceased father was part of some furry butt-fuck club, but, now, on a mission to find Horace's murderer, first they encounter this big weird church-like building in the woods, then they find a pile of very stinky boneless women, and now he had to worry about getting turned into a big lime.

"Clyde, I *gots* ta get out'a here. This place is just plain *evil.*"

"Just hold yer horses, brother," Clyde said. "Lemme do this first..."

Do WHAT? you might be asking.

Clyde had his dick back out and was urinating with liberality on the pile of boneless women. Each contributor to the pile squirmed in objection, flaccid arms and legs flapping, and they were all sort of mewling in that weird bleating sound they made.

"Gah! Gaaah! You-loo-loo-loo flat mluther-flugger!"

"Yoor-loor-loor muh-mluther slucks duh-donkey dlicks!"

"Bub-glub-grlub-blub!"

Clyde laughed and continued pissing, and you might say that he had a Super-Sized bladder, because even after two full minutes, the stream of urine showed no signs of abatement. Now he was deliberately directing the golden cascade into the jawless, gawping mouths of the girls, who began, of course, to involuntarily gargle the urine–"Lemme buy you ladies all a drink!"–and after *another* minute one or two of the girls drowned.

"Aw, come on, Clyde!" Gut yelled. "What'choo doin' that fer? Poor girls got it hard enough just bein' boneless'n all, and now you gotta *piss* on 'em too?"

"Hail yeah, Gut. Don't ya 'member what else Mr. Fitzwheeler say way back when in Sunday school? Ain't a woman born yet who didn't deserve ta be pissed on, and I mean pissed on *a lot.* See, Gut, the big secret is that all gals deep down *want* to be treated like shit. They *like* to be slapped silly, butt-fucked hard, punched in the kisser, kicked in the cunt, and, a'course, *pissed* on. Yeah, I know, it don't make no sense, but have you ever met a gal who does? See, unless you're whuppin' their asses one way or another, they ain't got no *self-esteem.* If you treat 'em *nice,* then they'll feel like they ain't worth nothin', like ya don't care 'bout 'em, which leave 'em with no choice but ta shit all over ya and make a perfect *asshole* out'a ya in front'a the whole blammed town. So's ya gotta give 'em one in the chops whenever ya can, or swing a ball-bat up 'tween her legs and give her cunny a great big howdy-do. Then's she get her self-esteem built back up'n she kin git back ta feelin' good about herself. Ya git what I'm sayin', brother? I done these boneless skin-bags a *favor* by peein' on 'em."

Gut could only stare in complete incognizance at his brother's wisdom (which would probably *not* be endorsed by the National Organization of Women), and he was getting quite adamant when he said, "Clyde, can we *please* git our asses *out* a this fucked up place?"

"In a minute, bro, in a minute. What say let's have us a little more fun with these boneless chicks?" Then he grabbed one by one of her flat-as-a-fried-egg tits, heaved her upwards, and started tossing her like pizza dough as she emitted a vocal objection like, "Guhlerup-plup-plup-plup!" Eventually he tired of this and threw her like a splat ball against the stone wall where she hung for a moment and then slid down into a heap. Then he grabbed another one (a redhead this time!), blew his nose in her face, and then commenced to twisting her entire body around like a great big wet rag. Next, he hauled up another girl ("Nuh-luh-no! Bleave mlee alur-own!"), grabbed one flaccid arm and held it out to Gut. "Take hold'a this here arm, Gut, come on, give it a squeeze. Ya can feel the muscles movin' 'round in there but no bone! Strangest damn thing ya ever felt! Like a snake slitherin' 'round *inside a stocking!*"

Gut threw his hands up. "Damn you, Clyde! You'll be fuckin' around in here all day! I'm leavin'!"

"No! No, wait! Look it this! I'll bet I can squeeze this gal's brain out her mouth! Watch!"

It was with great weariness and aggravation, then, that Gut halted his movement toward the exit and turned around.

Clyde still held the flaccid redhead, and now one of his hands gripped her around her throat while the other squeezed the sagging skull-less head. No longer within the containment of a skull, the brain did indeed began to bulge out of the unfortunate girl's mouth: a rare and spectacular sight.

"Ain't that sumpthin'?" Clyde celebrated, and then, for good measure, blew his nose in the redhead's hair, dropped her to the stone floor with a splat, walked back and forth on her a few times—also, for good measure—then headed for the basement's exit. All the while, the surviving boneless girls were bleating and blubbering incomprehensible obscenities behind him. "You ladies all have yerselfs a good day!"

Gut waited outside, relieved that he finally had access to breathable air. *Clyde's done et up with a case of the nutty ass,* he thought.

In another minute, Clyde joined him, wearing the expression of a man who'd just experienced a surplus of satisfaction. "Quit'cher lollygaggin', Gut, so's we can git back to the business'a findin' Horace's murderer." He glanced up the other side of the log-formed structure. "Come on, we ain't seen this side yet."

Both men huffed up the other side of the building. Gut suppressed his objection to that "lollygagging" remark, and he withheld any further objections. Whoever had killed Horace was long gone, and Horace (God rest his soul) had always been kind of a dick, and, brotherly blood or not, Gut would just as soon be back home working on a cold six-pack.

Clyde stopped halfway up the modest incline; he was leaning forward, squinting. "The hail's *that?* You see that, Gut?"

When Gut's attention span started, he peered ahead, was about to say "no," but then, dag-nabbit, he *did* see something, right up there next to the side of the building, and if he weren't mistaken, it seemed to be moving. "Is it a sack, or a bag, or somethin'?" Gut queried.

Whatever "it" was, it was a tannish color, or more like

khaki. And something about it seemed...jiggly. In fact, that "jiggle" seemed familiar...

"Blub-blub-blelp mlee!" the thing said.

Of course! It was another boneless person!

"But it's a fella this time," Clyde observed with little interest.

It was sort of spilling out of its clothes, hiking shorts and fancy fishing shirt. And the fancy suede boots looked stuck on to rubber legs. The man's head looked, well, pretty funny now that there was no skull to define its shape, and it was apparently a shaved head. This wobbly flat circle of the head looked like eyes, a nose, a mouth, and ears all floating in the puddle of fleshtone silly putty–really, a striking image, and more striking still when the awry mouth began to blabber: "Blub-blub-bleye need ub-ub-a-blamulace!"

"What's that, fella?" Gut asked.

"Said he wants a ambulance, I think," Clyde stated.

"Well, shit, Clyde. I'se guess we needs ta take him ta the harspital, huh?"

Clyde smacked his brother on the back of the head. "What's wrong with you, moe-ron! Git his wallet!"

Kneeling, Gut felt around in the boneless man's pockets and eventually pulled out a Saint Laurent snake skin designer wallet. "Holy shit! This fella's papered up!" Gut took out a sheaf of mostly $100 bills.

Clyde snapped that cash out of his brother's hand and pocketed it. "I'll hold that. Now check his ID."

Gut squinted at the plastic driver's license. "Looks like the fella's name is...Michael...Ling. And he from Los...Anjer-leese...California..."

Clyde huffed a great laugh. "Caaaaaalifornia! I never met *no one* from California worth more'n pinch of dick cheese." He leaned over and looked in Mr. Michael Ling's unsocketed eyes. "And, fella? Here's your ambulance..." Clyde planted his big booted foot into the middle of Ling's "face" and churned the boot around like someone putting out a cigarette.

There is no need to try and duplicate the sounds of outrage that Mr. Ling generated upon this act. However, Gut began to look more and more distressed. "Dang, Clyde, I'se startin' to feel kind'a upset 'bout all this."

"All this *what?*" Clyde gruffed.

"All this boneless business, ya know? I'se mean, what 'zactly could take all this fella's bones away, and all them stinky girls in the basement? It just ain't right, Clyde. It ain't *posserble.* I'se mean, what kin 'splain it?"

"Who gives a fuck?" Clyde hocked a great big hillbilly loogie into Michael Ling's warped mouth.

Gut worriedly shook his head. "More I think 'bout it–"

"So then *don't* think! You ain't got nothin' ta think *with!*" If you'se and a bucket'a pig shit took a I.Q. test, the bucket would win!"

"Come on, Clyde! More's I think 'bout all this, it seem to me the only explanation is ta say that somehow it were the *Bighead* that took all their bones."

Clyde stared right at his beloved brother and said, "If'n you don't stop yer yammering 'bout this Bighead nonsense, so help me, I will ball-bust you *so hard* that yer nuts'll swell all up to the size'a fuckin' canter-lopes like they did on that old man in the wheelchair who called us fat rednecks in feed-store parkin' lot that one time."

"But you said yerself that the Bighead were *shot* behind this place! You say that's what all the legends said! What-choo think 'bout *that?*"

"What I think, Gut? Well I'll tell ya what I think. I think it's all MALARKY!" Clyde shouted.

At this point, I'm very happy to say, the Bighead (who'd been standing on the roof) jumped down and in a proverbial split-second grabbed both brothers by the backs of their heads, then pushed their heads together face-first in what you might call the ultimate "french kiss." Their skulls crunched like styrofoam, one head gorily commingling with the other, brain mixing with brain, eyeballs popping against eyeballs, forming a great fancy-hued chunky jambalaya sort of mess that now existed between the Bighead's two huge hands.

Eight hundred pounds of dead-redneck meat hit the ground at the same time, and there was even a bit of a detectable tremor.

The Bighead stood there, nodding to himself, and he found considerable satisfaction in what he'd just done. It had been a day, in fact, full of gusto and stress-relief: first slaughtering all those high school soccer girls, and now this pair of obese, giant hayseeds. But, you know, his hands felt icky and he really wanted to wipe them off. But just as he would wipe them against the wood wall of the building, he looked down and, lo and behold!

There lay the jiggling, boneless remnants of Mr. Michael Ling from California. Bighead's big eye peered at this...thing, whatever it was. Now, his rapidly regenerating brain could formulate a postulation that it was indeed a person, but exactly what manner of person, the Bighead couldn't yet guess. The mass of flesh-colored slop did, however, seem to be wearing clothes, and you can bet those clothes were torn off with no delay, and then used to wipe off Bighead's hands. But something made Bighead do a double-take...

He couldn't help but notice the extraordinary *size* of Mr. Ling's dick. Of course, it wasn't as big as the Bighead's but it was probably half that size, and this no doubt made it the largest dick Bighead had ever seen on a human. Bighead was impressed.

He yanked it right off the boneless blob, balls and all, and winged in deep into the forest.

Ling's body–if you could call it that–convulsed vigorously, as if someone had dropped it on the third rail, and this is the best I can do in reciting Ling's vocal outrage: "Hug-uhg-oly fluckin' *shlit!*"

But the fun was not over yet. The Bighead got an idea. He picked up Mr. Ling like a great blob of hot taffy, and–

Well, let me give some thought as to how to phrase this...

You know how–if you're a male, at least–when your dick is at its very limpest, and with your index finger you can push down on your corona in such a way that your penis will actually *prolapse?* This action effectively turns the penis *inside-out* inside at the top of the scrotum. Come on. You know what I'm talking about. And any guy who says he's never done that...is a *liar.*

Anyway, this is pretty much what the Bighead did with Michael Ling...except, not with his corona (which was now lying forlornly deep in the woods) but with his *head.* That's right. The Bighead pushed Michael Ling's skull-less *head* down his neck, between his shoulders, then down, down, down until it started to squeeze out of his anus. This achieved, Bighead grabbed that bulb of weird flesh which protruded from the butthole, yanked on it, and in one great flapping motion, turned Mr. Ling's boneless body completely inside-out. Now all that was inside was visible outside: heart, aorta, lungs, intestines, etc.–the whole nine yards.

And like many things in this saga, it made for a *spectacular* sight, and if Bighead had had a cellphone he would've shot a selfie of him holding the prolapsed mass up like a trophy.

My! What a great day the Bighead was having, huh?

And it was about to get better...

The breeze shifted just then, and suddenly (we've observed this previously) there drifted to Bighead's preternaturally sensitive olfactory senses his absolutely *favorite* aroma, and what would that be? Of course:

Dirty pussy.

And this time it was, like, *real* dirty, so dirty that if a normal man had made the mistake of going down on it, he would *up and croak.* No exaggeration. Ah, but Bighead was not a normal man at all–he was a monstrous, sexually psychopathic hybrid–

and to him this stupefying, incognitable stench was as enticing as the aroma as someone's grandma's apple pie just out of the oven.

You can guess what happened next. Of course, Bighead followed the dirty-pussy stink back around to the rear of the building and found the hole knocked into the fieldstone. Now, this hole seemed to kindle something in the middle of Bighead's re-grown brain, a deja vu sort of thing. It was as if he'd seen this hole before, and this building too, some long time ago. But there was no time to contemplate the entails of this observation; indeed, that dirty-pussy aroma was just too strong. In fact, just from that smell in the air, his penis had already erected to its full twenty or more inches.

The Bighead squeezed himself through the hole and found himself standing in the midst of that glorious, pure, unadulterated stink, and when he looked deeper into the basement, we know full well what he saw. (Just as Bighead's sense of smell was super-sensitive, so was his vision, as I think has been previously mentioned.)

Those boneless, dirty creeker girls bleated and blabbered and jiggled away, and when the Bighead fully saw them he actually smiled. He was going to have himself a *good* ole time now...

* * * *

(I'll prelude here that though this novelist revels in describing shower scenes in books in which *women* are the ones taking the shower, there will be *no* describing *this* shower scene, in which the fat, old, fishbelly white *Writer* is taking a shower.)

The Writer stepped out of the shower and, rather sluggishly, began to dry himself, all the while staring open-mouthed at his own bearded face in the mirror.

I just arm-fucked a woman, he realized. *I ARM-fucked her.*

She'd begged him to do it, and what could he say after getting state-of-the-art fellatio from her, and then jizzed her tit like it was a fuckin' rum bun? What could he say? No?

She'd dragged herself and him right down to the floor with a surprising strength for a woman who must be in her forties. "Stick it in, *please,* stick it in!" she whispered. Horniness made her crosseyed.

"Uh, stick *what* in?" he'd asked, but then she'd simply showed him; she'd grabbed his hand and without much ceremony shoved it into that *gulch* of pink flesh that was her vaginal opening, then she grabbed his elbow and–WHAM!– slid his entire forearm in, and you can be sure there was no shortage of lubrication on Charity's part.

"Aw, fuck, that's good," she croaked, spreading her legs as wide as a gymnast's. At the top of the vaginal chasm, of course, showed that walnut-sized globe of her clitoris. This, she began to rub with one hand, while in the most dire tone of voice pleading, "Come on! Do it! You know!"

Well, the Writer most certainly did *not* know. He remained awkwardly poised on his knees and bending over in a manner most uncomfortable with his arm buried to the elbow in her, in her, in her...*giant pussy.* He imagined how he might look to a spectator, and then–far worse–he wondered if his dear departed parents were looking down from the heavens, shaking their heads in a way that said *Where did we go wrong?*

"Come on!" Charity yelled. "Back and forth!"

It was hard to put two and two together just then, but eventually he thought he got the message, and began to ease his forearm back and forth.

Charity tensed up. "Yes, yes, but faster! And make a fist!"

The Writer dizzily followed the orders, utilizing his forearm as something like a piston. Each time he pulled backward, her inner works exerted a surprising amount of resistance by way of a vacuum, and each time he pistoned forward, there was a great wet crinkling sound. And he could feel things in there too: first, all that slick flesh sucking against his forearm felt lot hotter than 98.6; in fact, if it got much hotter, he'd have to stop. There were an array of mysterious bumps, protrusions, pulsing veins, nubs, etc. Plus, he could swear there was something in there the size of a damn baseball–the G-spot, he could only suppose.

"Harder!" she yelled. "Faster!"

The next twenty minutes were thus consumed: the Writer's forearm banging in and out of her as hard and fast as he could; he might as well have been churning butter. Each time she experienced an orgasm, she tensed up, arched her back, shrieked, and released moans that were more like howls, and that channel of hot vaginal muscle spasmed and at times clenched his arm so tight it hurt.

This has got to end soon, he thought, already near exhaustion, still pistoning in and out, while the entire time Charily kept shrieking: "Harder! Faster!" So, harder and faster he went, in spite of his dwindling reserves of the energy.

"Lick that!" she bade him next, and of course she pointed to her ludicrously large clitoris, and when he commenced as commanded, Charity's sexual responses went into overdrive; the grand finale of her orgasms detonated. I really must leave to your imagination the extent of her wild utterances and her spasmodic body movements, and when the crisis was at an end, she lay asprawl on the floor like someone run over by a tractor-trailer.

It's about time, thought the Writer, relieved. When he pulled his arm out, the action begot a sound like pulling his arm out of a vat of raw, wet chicken parts, and to top it all off, once his arm had been fully extracted, several spectacular "cunt farts" crackled crisply in the air, as if to serve as the perfect accent to the three-ring clusterfuck circus that was now the Writer's life.

The aforementioned shower was immediately necessary, to wash off all that (sorry, no other term will do) pussy-juice. He felt like a man in his eighties while drying off, redressing, and trudging back out to the front parlor. Here Charity remained wiped out on the floor, cockeyed, tongue hanging out, and grinning idiotically. Tears glittered in her eyes when she panted,

"That was the best orgasm I've ever had..."

Orgasm? he couldn't resist the thought. *More like ARMgasm.*

"Great," he said, but suddenly a crappy mood sunk in.

Charity had finally gotten back up on the couch and re-covered herself with the towel, and this was just fine with the Writer because he was getting damn sick of looking at that giant fissure of a vagina. His arm had been elbow-deep in it just minutes ago, and this realization, now, struck him as a dream—a really *fucked up* dream—such that he wasn't even sure if he believed it. *The Bighead's twin sister,* he reminded himself, and that he *had* to believe.

But she had yet to be perfectly clear as to why she was here...

At once the odd quiet of the house was ruptured by the entrance of Dawn and Snowie, who barged through the front door, lugging a number of bags and packages. Both women looked stressed.

"Is there a T.V. here?" Dawn loudly inquired.

"Yeah, you gotta see the news," Snowie added.

"Well, as a matter of fact," the Writer said. He opened the armoire to reveal the big Sony. "But let's see if it works..."

Dawn gave Charity a sundress and flipflops they'd bought at the store. "Here's something to wear."

Charity lit up with delight. "Thank you! It's lovely!" She jumped up, dropped the towel, and slipped the dress on. "I'm gonna see how it looks!" She skipped off for the bathroom mirror.

Dawn's eyes went very wide, and she whispered, "Holy shit! Did you see the giant clit on that chick? I didn't notice it before."

It's not the only thing on her that's giant, thought the Writer, but he had no intention of reciting his recent actions. "So what's so important about the news?"

The T.V. picture had just fuzzed into focus, showing a news logo and grim video footage of a fenced compound in which EMT's were carting off bodies on stretchers. White sheets covered the bodies, and many of those sheets glared red with blood. "–when an unknown assailant, variously described as a monster and a giant, viciously attacked the Peasley High School girls' soccer try-outs at a training field near Luntville," came a very stoic female voiceover. At the same time a further announcement scrolled across the top: WORST MASS-MURDER IN STATE HISTORY. The Writer squinted in horror at the screen's details, and detected several young women in white lying headless and others limbless. Ropes of entrails looked stretched across the grass along with piles of what appeared to be whole human organs. One ironic severed head of a blond girl lay in the goal net.

"*Holy shiiiiit!*" exclaimed the Writer. "What the hell happened?"

"The Bighead went on a rampage, that's what," Dawn said. "He tore the fuck out of a shitload of high school girls playing soccer."

"I believe it," said the Writer, still staring. "There's nothing else that could've done all that."

Snowie indecorously scratched her ass, and then hitched her tits up in her t-shirt. "And that place ain't far from here."

Charity had returned and was watching too, but she didn't seem too surprised. "Bighead knows I'm alive; he can sense it just like I can sense him. But my gut tells me he's not coming here and not coming for me, at least not yet." She closed her eyes and shook her head. "At first I thought he might be, because I know he wants to kill me. He can't stand the thought of me, and he wants to fuck me to death. But now I'm feeling that it's not me he's on his way to."

The Writer didn't know how he felt about her speculation. "Then what *is* he on his way to?"

"The abbey," she answered. Her eyes looked diffuse. "Wroxton Abbey. An old Puritan church and rectory built in Colonial times. In the 1800s, it was purchased by the Catholic Diocese and used as housing for old priests and eventually a hospice and even a mental hospital for priests and nuns who became–"

"Fucked up in the head," Snowie offered.

"And, as you might've guessed," Dawn contributed, "the old townsfolk all swear it's haunted."

The Writer half-frowned. "I'm not terribly interested in ghosts, but I do want to know why the Bighead–after being dead in a morgue for twenty years and recently resuscitated– would want to go there?"

"Because that's the last thing he would remember. That's where he was killed, while trying to recover his father's corpse... *our* father's corpse."

The Writer, in spite of the story's convolutions, seized a defining question. "Why was the corpse there?"

"Townsmen killed it shortly after it raped our biological mother. They bricked it up in the basement of the abbey."

The Writer raised a finger. "And what exactly did they brick up?"

Charity shrugged. "Who knows? We only have the legend to go by, and the legend is split."

"Meaning, if the legend is true–" But here he paused in a subtle glee when he saw that Dawn and Snowie had remembered their instructions and purchased a case of Collier's Lager. He opened one with much anticipation. "If the legend is true then the Bighead's–and *your* father's–corpse was that of either an alien or a demon..."

Charity nodded resolutely. "And that's where I'm gonna have to go–the abbey."

"Sounds logical," said the Writer. "Which means..." He looked at Dawn.

"What!" Dawn barked. "I don't like that look!"

"The best idea is for you to say here, in the basement, and send the drone in, see if you can find Case."

"Fuck him and fuck you! I'm not staying in this fuckin' house by myself!"

An understandable complaint. "Okay, Snowie will stay with you and help, and Charity and I will go on to the abbey.

But first, let's try the drone."

"This I gotta see!" Snowie exclaimed with her long Lovecraftish face. She grabbed the big shopping bag and hastened toward the basement door, Charity right behind her.

But as the Writer was about to proceed, Dawn grabbed a fistful of his shirt and pulled him back.

"You fucked her, didn't you?"

"What?" the Writer asked. "Who?"

"Charity, that's who. Snowie and I were both betting that you'd be balls-deep in her the minute we walked out the door."

But the Writer didn't miss a beat with his lie, and used Bill Clinton's famous line, "I did not have sexual relations with that woman." He shook his head as if disappointed in Dawn. "You gotta get your head out of the gutter, Dawn. This is serious business going on here. People's lives are at stake. Fooling around isn't part of my plan." Then he winced a moment when he recalled the viscid image of Charity jerking him off on her tit and then swallowing his arm to the elbow with her vagina. *At the very least, I have an interesting life...*

Downstairs, the far door remained open (that door into which Case disappeared). Dawn explained, "I bought two drones 'cos there was a two-for-one clearance sale. The extra will come in handy if we lose one. And I bought a few extra capacity batteries. The guy at the store said they last forty-five minutes each but the battery that comes with each unit already has a half charge. That'll be enough for a trial run, and we'll charge all the other batteries in the meantime."

The Writer was impressed. "That's constructive thinking, Dawn."

"Of course. I was in the Army—we're resourceful and think ahead. How do you think we came up with using an embalming machine to inflate a dead guy's dick so we could get laid?"

The Writer opened his mouth but said nothing. He couldn't argue against her point. Snowie plugged all the batteries in, while Dawn assembled a drone on the table/altar which housed

Crafter's old grimoires and other sundry sorcerer items.

Charity seemed repulsed at first, examining the dead body of Pastor Tommy Ignatius which still hung impaled on another door. "This is a really screwed up room. It actually feels evil."

"It should," answered the Writer. "Many have been sacrificed here, impaled on the spikes in those doors in order to trigger an occult event, which in Pastor Tommy's case led to the opening of that far door."

"A door to Hell," Charity uttered, staring at it.

"I think so, yes, and we'll find out for sure momentarily."

Dawn's breasts jutted impressively as she held up a controller console and explained, "I got drones that came with separate controllers so I won't have to bother synching the unit into my cellphone. Everything the drone sees we see, on this little screen here"–a screen about the size of a large index card–"and we'll be able to hear too, 'cos the drone has a mike–it's known as a zoom mike, which projects forward so we won't hear much of the motor-noise."

"And you'll be able to record all that? The images *and* sound?" Charity asked.

"That's right. All the footage goes to an SD card in the controller, so even if we lose the drone, we still have the footage. But of course, there might not *be* any footage because we don't really know–"

"If a drone can even function in Hell," speculated the Writer.

"Yep. We'll find that out right now."

Dawn pressed a button on the controller, then the room filled with a tinny, almost annoying buzz. The small, four-propellered drone slowly rose off the table, paused in mid-air, then floated toward the open, lancet-shaped doorway at the end of the room...

"Here goes!" Dawn exclaimed.

...and then shot into it. The drone was gone in a second's time and so was the motor-sound.

The Writer, Charity, and Snowie all huddled behind to view the controller screen over Dawn's shoulder.

And this is what they saw:

Splotchy-black darkness with a dim rectangular splotch of dark-red light in the distance; as the drone proceeded, this rectangle grew larger. It grew larger rather quickly, suggesting that the passage between the door in the basement and the opening to Hell was not far. Then–

POOF!

Everyone lurched when the drone plunged into, first, red-tinted fog or steam, and then the open space of a vista impossible to describe. I, however, will describe it, bringing to bear my expertise as a quality author of fiction for nearly forty years standing.

They saw a city, or something like a city: a geometric demesne of impossible architecture which extended along a vanishing line of horrid black. They saw buildings and streets, tunnels and tower blocks, strange flattened factories whose chimneys gushed oily smoke. It was a necropolis, systematized and endless, and the sound coming through the little speaker was a terrifying, hollow *hooing* sound that must have been resonating from dozens or hundreds of miles away.

Essentially, what they were looking at was pandemonium. Gutters ran black with noxious ichor. Squat, stygian churches sang praise as if to mindless gods. A gust of wind screamed with human voices. Winged mites swarmed in the surreal air and burst into puffs of red mist when they had the misfortune of flying into one of the device's propellers.

"Make the drone fly higher," said the Writer. "Let's get a wider view of everything."

But as the drone gained altitude, it became clear that seeing "everything" was an impossibility. The drone's lens canted upward to show dim, drear-windowed skyscrapers at least a mile high. These cyclopean structures seemed to sway and lean at such extreme angles, the Writer thought they should topple at any moment, but didn't, as if they were subject to some anomaly of gravity or physics.

Twisted faces that couldn't possibly be human peered out of many of the narrow windows, while other windows were either broken out or spattered with blood. Sacks of skin hung out of other windows like sheets put out to dry, and on various window sills sat planter pots out of which grew things more like human sex organs than flowers. But more disconcerting than that was this: the sky visible between the buildings appeared to be red, and a black sickle moon hung in it.

"Holy fuck, it's true," Dawn muttered with pried open eyes. "That's no city on Earth. The only place it *can* be is Hell."

"My sentiments exactly," said the Writer. "Unless we're having shared hallucinations or *Folie à deux*, if such phenomenon are really possible."

"It's beyond belief," Charity whispered.

"I'm gonna have fuckin' nightmares!" Snowie shrieked, hugging Dawn.

Then all four of them yelled when a black bat with a six-foot wingspan and a vaguely human face glided past the drone; it looked over its leathery shoulder, smiled, and squeaked, "Fuck you!"

"Did that thing just say fuck you?" Dawn exclaimed.

The Writer's brows rose. "I do believe it did. Take the drone back down closer to the streets. Let's see if there are any people."

The drone buzzed and lowered, plummeting past window after window. In one window the Writer glimpsed what he thought was a curvaceous nude woman but with buttocks for a face, and it looked like she was about to defecate.

Finally the drone lowered to street level, and what a street it was. One sign read WELCOME TO ST. PUTRADA CIRCLE, HELL'S NEWEST FISTULATION & TRANSVERSION PREFECT. Another sign read, VAGINAL EXCISION ZONE: NOON - 2 P.M.

"What the *fuck* is that?" someone said.

"And what's *that?*" someone else yelled.

Yet another sign, this one posted next to several wheeled dumpsters, read PUS RECYCLING - 3 CENTS PER GALLON.

And then they saw people, or things *like* people.

They were more like monsters. Or were they combinations of both? A slim couple held hands as they strode by, flesh rotting from their limbs and faces. Several impish children wove through the crowd, with fangs like a dog's and eyes as big and as red as apples. A werewolf in a business suit and briefcase passed next, and he was followed by an attractive woman also in business attire, but from her hips sprouted arms such that she walked on her hands, and where her arms should be were of course legs. The woman looked at a wristwatch on her ankle, then quickened her pace. The watch had no hands on it. Next trotted by a fat clown with a hatchet in its face. It squeaked its rubber nose several times, looked right into the drone's camera, and said, "Hi, how are ya?"

"Fuck this shit!" Snowie blurted.

Just as anomalous as the living beings on the street were the vehicles. Cars that looked more like small steam engines chugged by on spoked wheels, as smokestacks up front gusted black-yellow soot and water vapor. Carriages and buggies rolled by as well, hauled along not by horses but by things *like* horses, whose flesh hung in dripping tatters. One carriage was occupied by a woman with skin green as pond scum who wore a tiara of gall stones and a dress made from tendons meticulously woven together. She fanned herself with a webbed, severed hand. In another carriage rode a creature that could've been a pile of snot somehow shaped into human form.

With her console controls, Dawn angled the lens back down and zoomed in on what appeared to be a row of ordinary vending machines from which one might buy a bottle of soda or bag of chips. But no such items were available here.

Instead, the slots behind the glass read: BABY TESTICLE ASSORTMENT - *3 ounces.* ASS HAIR - *2 packs for one!* ANGEL SWEAT - *genuine!* TROLL SMEGMA - *great on crackers!* The next machine boasted: USED RUBBERS - *1 Hellnote for empty, 3 for full.* CORPSE DANDRUFF & HEAD LICE MEDLEY - *1 pound bag!* EXCISED HUMAN VAGINAS - *fresh! 5 Hellnotes!* GARGOYLE BOWEL JUICE - *free with subscription!*

"I think we've seen enough of this, Dawn," the Writer said with a wince. "Drive the drone somewhere else." Just as the drone veered off they saw a final offering: MENSTRUAL CLOTS - *100 per sack! Better than jerky!*

Now the drone cruised straight down a lateral street–VASCULITIS BLVD, a sign stated–passing between more miles-high tenements, processing plants, and factories belching ill-colored smoke into the scarlet sky. On the street a Chinese restaurant became apparent, with flashing red neon tubes luring the attention of passersby. TODAY'S SPECIALS! CRISPY PEKING DICK! MOO GOO GAI BOWEL! GENERAL TSO'S BRAINS! EGG FOO PLACENTA! Most unsettling was a factory the size of a battleship; a great lit sign mounted over it read PUS RECYCLING CENTER #3,467,599. The girls seemed to watch in a shocked awe from the staggering images of the swaying buildings, but the Writer focused on the throngs of "people" moving to and fro on the sidewalks below.

These *pedestrians* were comprised by all manner of humans, demons, monsters, and diabolical hybrids. Some beings looked like they were formed with excrement, and many different types of horned beings walked side by side with winged beings. Here was a line of headless nuns, and there a cluster of naked, gray-skinned succubi, all grinning through blood-smeared mouths. Next, the Writer thought of Bosch's *Garden of Earthly Delights* when he espied a pregnant man with buttocks for a head and a pointed cap walking on legs like a goat's. Additionally, this figure brandished an erection and seemed to be in pursuit of a group of small monkeys with female human heads.

And next–

No, no! It can't be! the Writer thought.

Walking amidst the throng was none other than Elvis Presley. The Writer fumed. *No way! Elvis wouldn't be in Hell! It's got to be one of those impersonators...*

"Go down this next street," Charity advised, "where that statue of the Japanese guy is. I've got a hunch..."

"Might as well," Dawn said and steered the drone accordingly.

(The "Japanese guy" by the way, was a general of the Imperial Japanese army, Hideki Tojo. This wonderful fellow was responsible for turning most of Korea into a slave-and-rape camp and who initiated the slaughter of as many 14,000,000 Chinese, just so the Japanese army would have plenty of rice to eat. The guy kind of made Hitler and Himmler look like Mickey and Goofy.)

The drone buzzed down a smokey street lined with 10-foot-high poles on which naked humans–mostly women, regrettably–had been impaled. But the biggest problem with this was the evidence that, in Hell, humans couldn't die, which definitely sucked for these women. The damned naked bodies just writhed, twitched, and quivered on their eternal stakes.

But even more shocking was the edifice that appeared at the end of this infernal street:

An immense mansion following the lines, contours, and architectural patterns of homes of the Victorian era, highlighted by turrets, cupolas, dormers, gables, great bay windows, and a myriad of stained glass. But this is where structural similarities ceased and diabolic anomaly took over. What I mean is, the house was not constructed with the standard building materials of the day. It was made, instead, entirely with human heads.

Imagine, in other words, a brick wall but each "brick" was a human head severed just above the adam's apple, and some manner of hellish mortar cemented them together. Of course, some heads had to be trimmed in half or in smaller slivers–as one would trim tiles to get them to fit–so that they could serve as embrasures for door and window frames.

Yes. The giant multistoried house was built with human heads. And one more detail: the heads were all still alive. They blinked, yelled, yawned, screamed, and even conversed with one another. An iron fence encircled the estate, and above its entrance crest were the words LE DIABLE MANIORE.

"Manse Lucifer," the Writer said. "It's mentioned in *Unaussprechlichen Kulten* by von Juntz, an ancient German warlock. It's the Devil's house."

Snowie shivered and squealed. "Let's quit this scary shit! I wanna go home and smoke some bud and get shit-faced!"

"That's not a bad idea," Dawn said, "and I need to bring it back now anyway 'cos the battery's low. It only came with a partial charge."

"Do you remember how to get it to come back here?" asked the Writer.

"Don't have to. All I gotta do is push the return button. The navigational chip remembers the starting point. The drone will come right back here."

But before Dawn could press the button, Charity exclaimed, "Look at that! Do you see that guy there? It looks like he's climbing the wall!"

The Writer squinted at the small screen. But–yes!–a man was climbing in zig-zag fashion up the front wall off the house, wedging the tips of his shoes into the mortared seams between the heads. Some of the heads even seemed to be talking to the climber but the drone couldn't quite pick up the talk.

"Looks like he's heading for that open window on the third floor," Dawn observed. "But I gotta get the drone back before the battery craps out."

"Wait!" yelled the Writer. Now the drone had edged a bit closer, and they could see better details of the man climbing. He was wearing black slacks and a black shirt, for instance.

Then he inadvertently turned his face toward the lens.

"It's Case!" Snowie exclaimed.

And indeed it was, but he didn't seem to take note of the drone.

"Get in a little closer," the Writer instructed.

Dawn shook her head. "If I don't bring the drone back now, it's never coming back." She pushed the return button. The four-propellered machine turned hard and began to buzz back the way it came.

"At least we know where he is," the Writer said. "Can you remember how to get back to Manse Lucifer?"

"It's only two turns out the portal door," Dawn said. "I should be able to find it again easy."

"But why the hail would Case wanna sneak into the *Devil's* house?" Snowie asked with some alarm.

The Writer crossed his arms in thought. "I have a feeling Case plans to embark on a little Christian soldiering."

"Like, what?" Dawn said, "he's gonna go in there and kick the Devil's ass?"

"I wouldn't be surprised if he was entertaining an idea of that nature. It's hard to doubt the faith of a man who cuts off his own tattoos as a means of repentance. But all that aside, once the high capacity batteries are fully charged, you'll have to take the drone back in and try to get his attention."

"I'll tie a note to it, saying it's us," Dawn suggested. "I'll tell him to follow the drone back here."

"Excellent idea," the Writer approved. "But of course, by the time the new batteries are charged and you get the drone back there, Case probably will have already gotten inside of Manse Lucifer. So you'll have to fly the drone in there too."

"No problem," Dawn said. "I'd love to see inside that place."

"Not me!" Snowie blurted. "We might see the Devil!"

Dawn smirked. "Where's your sense of adventure?"

The Writer intervened. "Just get on that as soon as the batteries are charged. And while you're doing that...Charity and I will be investigating Wroxton Abbey..."

* * * *

Meanwhile...

Let us not forget our two Mafia friends, Paulie and Augie. Augie now sat hugely behind the wheel of their black Lincoln Town Car with the "suicide doors," cruising determinedly through Luntville and beyond, eventually hitting a ribbony stretch of asphalt called Governor's Bridge Road.

"How much farther, Aug?" Paulie asked, sitting aside in the passenger seat.

Augie checked his phone. "Looks like just a coupla more miles, boss, according to this GPS thingie. It's gonna be some surprise when we walk in on those two cunt-carriers."

"Yeah. Still can't believe the balls on those bitches, blowing off *our* calls all day. They think they can make a fool'a me, they got another thing comin'. Remember, we do a job on 'em like what we done on that stoolie's daughter in Scarsdale. First we blowtorch their assholes, then we blowtorch their pussies, then we blowtorch their faces. And film the shit, too, of course." Paulie nodded in the contemplation. "And I might have to belly-fuck the albino, give her some of the good ole Italian cock sauce right in the tum-tum."

Augie chuckled. "Yeah, boss. That squawkin' funny-face bitch deserves it. And if the Army gimp is still alive after I flame-broil her face, I'm thinkin' I'll strangle her with her fake leg."

Paulie clapped and busted a laugh. "Now that's what I call thankin' her for her service!"

But a quite unexpected sound severed the reverie, a loud BANG! It sounded, in fact, a bit like a .38 round going off very close to them. Paulie yelped and drew his piece! "Fuck, Augie! Is this a hit?"

But Augie remained cool as a cucumber (however cool that is), and said, "Naw, boss, relax. It's just a flat tire. Won't take me 10 minutes ta fix."

The standard *plap! plap! plap!* sound was heard from a rear wheel. Augie slowly pulled over onto the shoulder, which was flanked by dense woods on a vast incline. Then he got out, popped the trunk, and commenced to retrieving the jack and spare tire. Meanwhile, Paulie checked his voice-mail to see if maybe the two jizz-buckets had called back, but, no, they hadn't. Paulie smiled and flexed the meager boner in his pants when musing upon the treats those girls had waiting for them. He was getting sick of them anyway, and, yeah, while it was true the pegleg's mortuary was a perfect place to shoot corpse-sex, he was getting sick of that too. It was time to move on to new horizons, and what with the Dark Web opened up, there was a lot of Bitcoin waiting to be picked up by the entrepreneur who came up with the next Big Thing in underground porn. Paulie had some ideas flitting around his polluted head.

Snuff-sex with retarded kids? he thought. *Nursing homes? Yeah! Send some boys in at night and set some old people on fire and film it! And fuck the shit out'a any nurses who happened to be good-lookin'!* But it was hard thinking of new stuff for the market; it had all been done before. *Skinning jobs, sledgehammer jobs, steam-roller jobs. That shit's old hat these days. Shit, maybe we should start filmin' home-invasions, rape the wives and daughters, machete the dads and boys, and have everyone doing the gig wear body cams with infrared. Fuck, people would buy that in a heartbeat.* Then another idea sparked: *Ooo, ooo, this is even better! Steam-rollers have been done to death but I ain't never seen no one steam-roll PREGNANT CHICKS! Stake 'em spread-eagled on the ground, then roll over 'em slow, head-first! I'll bet the fetuses'd pop right out their pussies and shoot ten feet! That's a sure seller on the web!*

Such was the gist of thoughts that occupied Paulie's mental processes while he waited for Augie to do the tire. But come to think of it...

He had yet to hear Augie make a sound.

Paulie jumped out and headed toward the rear of the car.

"Hey, Aug. Let's get this show on the road, huh?"

But then he stopped mid-stride. There was the flat tire on the car, and there was the trunk opened, but where was Augie? He should be standing there right now getting the jack and spare, and there should be noise to accommodate that fact.

But there was no noise, and no Augie.

Paulie was getting ticked. *It ain't like Augie ta fuck around...* Perhaps he'd stepped out into the woods to take a piss, but... No, Augie wouldn't've wasted the time. He'd pee right there in the street.

At the same moment Paulie was about step around to the rear of the car, he did indeed hear a sound.

But it was like no sound he'd ever heard.

"Blub-bluh-BLOSS! Glug-glug-glug...GLET OUT!"

Paulie jerked his gaze down, his eyes bugging. "Augie! The fuck?"

What Paulie saw, as we may have guessed by now, was his good friend and right-hand man reduced to a state quite unlike anything Paulie had observed in the entirety of his jaded life.

Augie was *collapsing* in place. The sturdy legs he'd always stood on had turned to putty, as though he were a big Italian wax doll, and as the man beseechingly reached out to his boss, his brawny arm slowly bowed and flopped into a total loss of turgidity.

"Damn, Augie! What happened, man? Who did this too ya?"

Now, Augie's *head* seemed to be losing shape. "Muh-muh-mly fluckin' blones are fluckin' mlelting. Wuh-la-was-thlem tloo blitches..."

"Two...*what?* Two bitches? You mean the Gimp and Fugly?"

Augie's head was sinking into the midst of his now collapsing shoulders. "Nuh-nuh-nuh-nuh no, bloss. Luh-luh ill-ill-ill...it wuh-lus-was tloo guh-glirls iiiiiin bub-bub-bub...black..."

Two girls in black? What the fuck was he talking about?

"Aug? What the fuck?" It was here that Paulie took one

last look at his royally fucked up friend, who by now had been reduced to 250-pounds of flesh-slop encased in a charcoal gray Brioni suit. Paulie, not a mental powerhouse to begin with, began to experience some manner of brain-function overload. Bones melting? Two girls in black? What girls? And where were they?

Just then, a voice, or something *like* a voice, fluttered behind him, and said:

-hello? oh, hello! don't you want to kiss us?-

Paulie's face began to pale when he heard this voice. A strange voice it was indeed. He seemed to have heard it more in his head than with his ears. Then his face turned completely white when he looked behind him and saw—

You gotta be fuckin' kiddin' me...

—two young women in black cloaks and hoods standing at the woodline on the other side of the road. They wore sunglasses, and their mouths seemed to be glossy scarlet.

And their faces were white. Perfect pure untainted white. And one more thing: both women seemed to be wearing pendants around their necks, pendants of upside-down crosses.

-come here- their silly little-girl voices throbbed in Paulie's head. *-let us kiss you! you'll like it!-*

That was about it for Paulie. He jumped in the Lincoln, started the engine, and floored it—flat tire be damned. The big car fish-tailed, rubber squealing, flat tire flap-flap-flapping on the asphalt. Conscious thoughts were not now occupying Paulie's head. Where was he going?

Anywhere but there.

The car buckled down the road at breakneck speed, through one bend after another. But Augie's cellphone lay on the seat, and suddenly it started talking:

"Your final destination is approaching. Turn left in a quarter mile."

It was that GPS thingamajig that Augie turned on to find out where the gimp and the albino were. In another minute: "Turn left and stop. You have reached your destination."

Paulie turned left and stopped. Clearly, the Lincoln wouldn't be able to go much farther on the flat. But what he parked in front of was a dirt entrance way, and on one side sat a blazing white Chevy El Camino. Paulie parked next to it, gun drawn, on the lookout for anymore of those fucked-up looking women in black. A glance into the El Camino showed him no keys in the ignition. *The girls must have them...* He knew he had to get *far* away from here as fast as possible.

A foliage-lined path led up a hill, and at the end of the path, he could see the roof of an old house. Driving up wouldn't work because the path was just a foot trail, not wide enough, so Paulie began to hoof it.

His heart pounded. He heaved in breath. A high iron gate stood at the top of the incline but it hung open. Still half in shock, Paulie stepped through and found himself looking at a dilapidated three-story mansion, Victorian in style. *A dump, a hovel,* he thought. *Why would that pair of redneck fuck-ups be HERE?*

Paulie wasted no time. He ran for the house.

* * * *

Since the Writer had no idea where he was going, he followed Charity down the slope behind Crafter's house and then into a wooded trail. Case's car–an older black Mercedes four-door–sat down behind the hill.

As a writer, he tried to appreciate all this natural beauty about him: these ancient woods unblemished by ax blades and chainsaws, garlands of venerable vines deliriously green, centuried trees standing a hundred feet and higher, and above, the golden sunlight streaming down from a limpid sky through the magnificent overbrush. Yes, these were visions that most writers would crave to examine, and to put into their own terms creatively.

Most writers, yes, but not *our* Writer.

His examination had limited itself to Charity's shapely ass swaying back and forth in the summer dress. *Damn, that ass could launch a carrier group, and I really wouldn't mind seeing those bare tits again.*

But why did these lewd thoughts persist? With all that had transpired thus far, sex should be the furthest notion from his mind, right? He'd seen a monster-wrought massacre of school girls on the local news, he'd seen a genuine demonic possession, he'd seen a dead man buried for years run into the house, and now he'd seen live video footage of Hell. Earth-shattering events such as these should reduce sexual daydreams to utter frivolousness.

Charity glided down quite briskly on the dollar-store flipflops the girls had picked up. The Writer trundled behind, clumsily toting a plastic bag which contained a bottle of beer and the big antique pistol. Charity looked back over her shoulder several times, then stopped and turned.

"Am I walking too fast for you? We can rest if you want."

The Writer had been concentrating on her backside so intently that he didn't realize he was out of breath, and he frowned at her observation. *Makes me feel like a fat old man... which I am...*

She sat down on a log and bade him to join her. This, of course, sparked his Pervert Meter, and as he sat down beside her, it was his natural instinct to look down the rather low swoop of the top of her sun dress and get a, shall we say, a gander of Tit City. He sat down slow to maintain that delectable image. But the moment he did seat himself on the log, Charity automatically took his hand. The Writer's reaction? Instant erection.

"I've been thinking," she said, gazing out into the plush woods, "about what we were talking about earlier, you know, the legend."

Periodically, she squeezed his hand as she talked, and each squeeze caused his erection to throb. His thoughts were difficult to organize. "Uh, oh, you mean the question of genetics?"

"Yes. The legends don't clarify. One says the Bighead is part-alien, and the other says he's part-demon, and that goes for me too because I'm his twin. I've thought about that question every day for twenty years."

"You mean, do you have alien genes or demon genes?"

"Exactly."

"So after twenty years of contemplation, have you come to any conclusion?"

She gazed right at him with depthless eyes. "Why not both? Maybe I'm *both,* and the Bighead is too."

The Writer was getting hot under the collar now, being this close to her, his hand in hers. *Fuck. What did she say? Both?* "In other words, you're wondering if aliens *and* demons comprise part of your genetic heritage?"

"Yeah. Why not?"

"Well, that's an interesting question to say the least, and a loaded one. Modern philosophers revel in such considerations. But it can't be addressed until some sort of baseline is recognized..." The Writer desperately needed to distance his awareness from Charity's sensuality, and here was a way that might succeed in that. "First, is there God or is there no God? Many mathematicians claim to have proved the existence of God but it's still all just complicated subjectivity that *no one* can perceive unless they happen to be mathematical geniuses on the same level as Leibniz, Einstein, and de Sitter. But one communal agreement seems to be the affirmation that if there *is* God, then there must also be a Devil. Likewise, if there's a Heaven, then there must be Hell. And we have some inroads on that prospect, don't we?"

She stared open-eyed at him, her lips parted. "We saw Hell, in that basement, on the drone screen."

"Yes, we did, and at this point I am willing to accept no other conclusion," the Writer said. "That was *Hell.* A real place.

Not a figment of mutual suggestion, not hallucination, not radon gas in the walls–no. It was genuinely *Hell,* the home of *Lucifer,* the Prince of Darkness. And since we've now established that the home of Lucifer exists, so, too, must Lucifer himself. And since we believe that Hell exists, then we must, according to the baseline, believe that Heaven does as well. If Hell exists, so then must Lucifer, and if Heaven exists, so must God. Do you agree with that?"

Still staring, still gripping his hand, she nodded.

"So do I. Ah, but that doesn't really help answer *your* question, does it? Alien or demon, or could it be both? To me, this conundrum is much more interesting. Astrophysicists argue endlessly, half convinced that God can't possibly exist, the other half just as convinced the God *must* exist. A supreme, sentient creator, these latter say, is the *only* explanation for Earth's existence and therefore the existence of the human race. We're told by the Bible that God created the universe in six days. Is this abstraction? Is this just a metaphor? I don't know, but here's what I do know: what we just saw on the drone screen was the genuine Biblical Hell. But on the other hand, boundless archaeological observations suggest that God is not really a divine entity, but an *alien* one. And this addresses your own personal reflection: why not both? If God created the world then He must've created *other* worlds, and the inhabitants of those worlds would be what? We would have to think of them as *aliens.*" The Writer shrugged. "I've got no problem with that, and I don't think you should either. There's no reason to limit ourselves to the black and white. We know there's something bigger than us out there, because we just saw half of it back in Crafter's basement. Humans don't have the intellectual capacity to understand all of it. It just *is.* God is the creator of *all* worlds, and if that's true, then Lucifer is His antithesis in all those other worlds as well. Therefore, in my opinion, at the end of the day...it's all good. It doesn't matter if you're part-alien or part-demon. And you may well be both. I may be, we all may be. The only thing that matters is that we all, simply, *are*."

Charity smiled, and seemed quite relieved by that thesis, but the Writer knew he'd just been reeling off some introspective claptrap so that he could keep half an eye on the shape of her breasts in the sundress top. *What I wouldn't give to have my face in that rack one more time,* came the cringing thought. And certainly, judging by her attitude, how close she was sitting to him, and her hand squeezing his, that prospect seemed very doable. However, the Writer knew he must buck up, and do the most responsible–and the most boring–thing.

"So, with all that in mind, let us continue with our trek to...whatever awaits us..." He helped her up, cast a final glance down her cleavage, and continued to follow her down the trail. A few moments later, she seemed to half-stumble and pointed down. "Watch out for that thing. I almost tripped over it."

The Writer stepped up, looking down. "That's weird. It looks brand-new." What he referred to was a hefty, two-foot-long monkey wrench, with a bright-red handle. "Looks like a plain old everyday monkey wrench."

With an appropriate expression, she asked the logical question. "Why would there be a *monkey wrench* sitting here in the middle of nowhere?"

"Haven't a clue," the Writer said, and then they marched onward. *Could a workman have dropped it?* he wondered. *Pretty big thing to drop and not notice, and what would a workman be doing out here?*

Charity stopped again and exclaimed, "And what the heck is this big box doing here?"

Big box? The Writer could not possibly resist the joke. *Oh, you mean the big box between your legs?* but then he felt an instant shame at the thought. He approached with a furrowed brow, and, sure enough, there was a big cardboard box sitting amongst the weeds at the side of the path. It was sealed with brown mailing tape but had no address on it, and the box itself looked, like the wrench, brand-new.

Charity started, "Do you think we should…"

"Why the hell not?" The Writer bent over, ripped off the mailing tape, opened the box, and stared.

"You're kidding me!" Charity said.

What the box contained, also in a brand-new state, was (have you guessed already?) a kitchen sink.

Oh, boy. He sheepishly looked at Charity. "Let's forget about this and the monkey wrench, and just keep going."

"But, seriously," she complained, "why on Earth would a *brand-new kitchen sink* be sitting here in the woods!"

"Surely, we'll never know, so let's move on," and then he took her by the elbow and goaded her back down the trail. He had a sinking feeling that the sudden presence of a monkey wrench and a kitchen sink, in the middle of deep West Virginia woods, presaged something, well…something not right, and now he was beginning to smell a great big aesthetic rat. *Best just to leave it alone…*

He tried to sway his attitude more positively, regarding this as an adventure. Why did she feel it necessary to go to this Wroxton Abbey? But he figured it made sense to trust her instincts. *After all, she IS the Bighead's twin sister.* "Is it much farther?"

"Less than a mile, I think," she said, marching resolutely ahead. But then she slowed in a strange manner and moved her opened hand back. "Wait, look." She stopped. "People."

The angle of the sinking sun and the position of the path in the trees allowed the sharp black silhouette-shapes of two approaching figures. At once, the Writer thought of James Dickey's *Deliverance,* and imagined, with some genuine terror, of being forced at knife-point to suck hillbilly cock a few moments from now, but then he remembered he had the big clunky pistol in his bag. At any rate, the Writer's fears evaporated when the pair of figures revealed themselves to be two park rangers in the expected green and tan garb and Smokey the Bear-type hats, one a tall, bearded, dark-eyed man, and a lissome but well-breasted woman with Indonesian looks.

"Howdy, folks," greeted the man, "no needed to be alarmed. I'm Ranger Gemser and this is my partner Ranger Eastman. Looks like you two are out for a nice hike."

"That's right," said the Writer. "Appreciating such spectacles of nature."

Then Charity added, "And we want to take a look at Wroxton."

"Oh, well, you need to be real careful out there," said the woman, Ms. Eastman. "Not a good idea to go inside—it's so old it's fit to collapse."

"We were just going to look around the outside," the Writer said, letting one eye take note of the fact that Ms. Eastman had forgotten to put on her bra this morning, and those tight ranger-pants seemed to be sporting some serious "Camel-Toe."

"Oh, that's just fine, sir," Ranger Gemser said, "but try to stay out of the brush. This great state of ours is loaded with ticks, snakes, chiggers, and what not. And if you don't mind my asking, are you armed?"

The Writer froze. *Am I about to get arrested for having a gun with no permit?* Both rangers had stout automatics on their hips, as one would expect. But then the Writer thought, *Wait a minute, this is West Virginia. They practically sell handguns in vending machines here.* He held up his plastic grocery-store bag. "Yes, I've got a revolver, for self-defense, of course."

"Well, that's good, sir," the man said, "just in case you haven't heard about the tragedy earlier today."

"Yeah," the woman jumped in, "not too far from here there was a massacre of dozens of high school girls, and the perpetrator is still at large."

Charity nodded. "The description on the news of the

carnage made it sound like a ferocious animal attack–"

Ranger Gemser looked grim. "Yes, it did, but the crazy thing is that all the witnesses say it was the work of just one man–a very *big* naked man, if that isn't the nuttiest thing."

Yeah, we know all about it and even know who the killer is, thought the Writer. *And wouldn't you find it interesting that the murderer's twin sister is standing right here?* "You can bet we'll be very careful, officers, and if we see anything suspicious, we'll call 911 at once."

"Great," said the male ranger. "You all have a nice day."

The rangers moved along, and Charity and the Writer continued down the trail. "That does bring up an interesting point," the Writer said.

"And what's that?"

"We know that the orchestrator of the slaughter was the Bighead. The rangers warned us to be on our guard. What are we going to do if the Bighead suddenly appears before us?"

Charity strode along confidently, her flipflops crunching twigs. "Well, if that happens, run. The Bighead will be coming for me, so use that distraction to get away."

"You want me to *abandon* you?"

"Yes. No reason in both of us dying, but that'll probably happen anyway. If you can get a clear shot at him with your pistol, *don't* aim for his body–his muscles will just push the bullet out. Aim for his eye or his ear canal, or his mouth if it's open; there's less bone to stop the bullet. The guy who originally killed the Bighead two decades ago was a priest named Thomas Alexander. He got a lucky shot right in the Bighead's smaller eye, and that did the trick; blew a bunch of my brother's brains out the back of his head."

The Writer considered this with little confidence. A marksman he was not. "What happened to the priest?"

"He died of a heart attack the next day."

"Bummer."

"But, seriously, if Bighead surprises us, just run, I won't mind," she said, still marching along, looking straight ahead. "I have a trick or two up my sleeve."

Sounds like a faulty quip to me, the Writer couldn't help thinking. *She's not wearing any sleeves...* "Really? Such as?"

She didn't reply but said instead, "I think this is the place..."

Bulky shadows between the trees up ahead eventually transformed into a long man-made structure, something like a big log cabin. Closer, the Writer noticed that most of the place was festooned with vines and ivy, and it sat upon a stone foundation. Narrow stained-glass windows were visible, but their thematic depictions were not, due to so many years of mold, fungus, or simply being broken.

"Refresh my memory. It's your belief that the Bighead is coming here, for...*what* reason?"

"Like I said, it's where he died. This place is the last thing he'd remember before that happened."

"What a dismal place to die," the Writer muttered, "even for a monster." He looked more closely at the decrepit building's details. "But where, like *exactly*, did this happen? Inside the abbey?"

"No, it was out back by the lake, but it wasn't really a lake. More like a big pond or swamp; I think it was man-made. But it's dried up now. Let's look."

He followed her down the slight incline, the bottom of which revealed the full height of the back fieldstone wall. The angle at which they stood precluded their noticing the hole that had been knocked into that wall decades previously. The Writer then followed her farther down, via a trail, and couldn't help but notice...

"That must be the lake," he said, "but...is it really dried up? What's with all the fog over the surface?"

Charity examined the sight with some confusion. "That's a surprise. I guess it's ground fog or swamp gas or something.

I suppose some water could've drained back into it after all these years."

It was a strange ovalish perimeter that they viewed, not really a lake but a sizeable pond covered with fog, and the fog seemed ill-colored. It all sat a ways behind the abbey's rear wall, and was nestled in a picturesque recess of very tall trees. They followed a winding trail down but both stopped abruptly upon noticing the same thing...

"You're shitting me," the Writer muttered.

"Fuck," Charity said. "Are those *limbs?*"

They were—no question about it—limbs: two legs disconnected at the hips, and two arms apparently *yanked* from the shoulders—all lying scattered near the lake's meager shore. If this weren't anomalous enough...

"These aren't just limbs," observed the Writer, now down on one knee for closer observation, "they're *fucked up* limbs..."

Both legs wore shiny black boots up to the knees. The thighs were bare and, like the arms, they were whiter than the Writer had ever noticed human skin being, even Snowie's.

Bloodless, he thought, but now that he'd brought the idea to his attention, there was not a drop of blood anywhere. Even if this person had been dismembered elsewhere, there'd be some infinitesimal trace of blood. And the arms were the same way, a *whiteness,* that was absolute, like new snow. He picked up a leg and Charity picked up an arm, each making their own inspections. *What the HELL is this?* he thought, looking at the flesh of where the leg had been torn from the body. But it wasn't flesh, and what ordinarily would've been the upper-arm bone—the humerus—was only a black rod, a Tinker Toy's width. "Are you noticing what I'm noticing?"

"There're no real bones in these limbs. They're just sticks," Charity said. "And no muscles, either, and no veins or arteries, only—"

"Red threads? Are these capillaries?"

It was true. The severed "leg" in the Writer's hand bore no kinship to any leg he could ever imagine. One might think of it as a tube of white clay supported by a thin black stick down the middle. But amid this curious white matter that existed where muscle should be, the Writer noticed myriad red dots and when he pinched one of those dots he pulled on it, he withdrew some sort of red thread-like strand. "What the hell is going on? Are these mannequin limbs?"

"One thing's for sure," Charity said, "they're not human limbs."

"Yeah, and we need to find the torso they used to be connected to. But where is it?"

The question was answered after only a few minutes of meandering around weeds by the shore. First, a pair of sunglasses was found and close by lay a shiny black cloak with a hood.

"This is more fucked up by the minute."

"How's this for fucked up?" Charity said.

She was pointing down, not to a dismembered torso but to a pendant on a chain, which wouldn't be terribly odd save for the fact that pendant connected to the chain was an upside-down cross.

"Interesting," remarked the Writer, "and, yes. Fucked up." He picked up the pendant, which was silver or like silver, and as it turned it gleamed in the lowering sun. That gleam seemed to generate a spark of headache, so he put the cross and the sunglasses in his bag. "I guess I can understand someone around here dropping a pair of sunglasses...but not an upside-down cross. Creepy is not quite the word for this."

"Here's something a bit more creepy, I think," Charity offered, now pointing to something else.

It was a collapsed severed head. Details were difficult to identify (because the head looked caved in) but there was evidence of long shiny black hair attached to chunks of skull—however, no brain matter could be discerned between said

WHITE TRASH GOTHIC 3

chunks, just more of the white clay-like substance. Pressure had ejected the eyeballs, which were nothing but black orbs. There also appeared to be a squashed mouth: red-lipped almost as if garish lipstick had been applied, and teeth more canine than human. But less explicable than any of this was what seemed to hang out of the remnants of the mouth. Not a tongue, as one would normally expect, but a–

"What the fuck is *that?*" questioned the Writer with some annoyance. "Is that supposed to be a tongue?"

That was a long pink squiggly thing, akin to a thin, dead snake, maybe a quarter-inch wide and ten feet long.

"I don't know *what* it's supposed to be," Charity said, "or *any* of this."

The Writer picked up a stick and used it to fiddle with the supposed tongue; he half-expected it to slither to life, whereupon he would no doubt shit his pants, but the pink, snake-like thing only hung limp off the stick. Its terminus tapered down to a meaty cone that seemed to have a sharp barb sticking out of it.

The discoveries over the past minute were too much to process; neither the Writer nor Charity were thinking rationally just yet. The Writer squinted down at the insane conundrum and said, "We're not quite comprehending what this really is, are we?"

Charity, open-mouthed, shook her head no.

"And we've both *got* to be thinking along the same lines..."

Charity nodded her head yes.

"These body parts are *real.* They're not pieces of department store dummies, they used to be *living things* but, but–"

"Not living *human* things," Charity uttered. "Which means they can only be alien."

Thank God she said it before me... "Right, and if they're not aliens in the science-fiction sense, then they must be demons, in the occult sense, and that's an interesting coincidence considering what we discussed before."

"That it might be both," she said, "or that both elements are at play here."

"Exactly...*if* we're going to accept the possibility of such things, which I do." The Writer looked around in frustration and began stepping forward. "But where the hell is the torso? *That's* what I want to see. It must be close." Just then, his foot caught on something and over he went. *Fuck! I'm too old to fall down!* But what had he tripped on? A root? A rock?

No. A torso.

"There it is," Charity said. But when she leaned over to help him up, the Writer didn't even look down her top this time.

There was the torso, lying in some weeds. Much like the head, it was squashed. The ragged stumps at the shoulders, hips, and neck were obvious and showed the same mysterious white clay-like material, dotted by tiny red threads. The victim, indeed, was female, for a pair of breasts were evident on the chest, breasts that any man might describe as "bodacious" except for the fact that they *entirely lacked nipples*. And where the vagina would be there was no sign of pubic hair, nor labia, nor clitoris. It was just a smooth, blank-white bump. But even more interesting than that was the undeniable *footprint* in the middle of it, and it was an *immense* footprint.

"Well, I don't think we have to guess," the Writer said. "The Bighead did this."

Charity's reaction to this assertion seemed in doubt but... maybe the Writer's imagination was causing him to misconstrue his powers of observation...

Finally, Charity said, "You've seen the Bighead, right? We both have. His feet are huge but...are they *that* huge?"

The question seemed odd. He looked closer at the massive impression on the torso. It was that of a bare humanoid foot but *very* large. However, a better impression could be seen just one step up from the torso, in some semi-dry mud.

"The Bighead's got to be eight-feet-tall and then some,"

the Writer said, stooped over. "But...the print is over three-feet long. When I saw the Bighead's body on the mortuary table...I don't think his feet were that big." He stroked his bummy-looking beard. "What do you make of that? You think there's something even *bigger* than the Bighead that did this?"

Charity's eyes leveled on his but all she said was, "Let's look closer at this swamp or lake or whatever it used to be."

The Writer followed her down, not comfortable with the idea that something even bigger than the Bighead might be around.

That uncommon fog just lay there on what would be the surface of the water but, then, there supposedly *was* no water since the swamp had drained years ago. This time, when Charity bent over, the Writer did indeed look down the front of her top to visually revel in the image of her succulent, depending breasts. *Sweet Mother of Ariadne, that's a pair of exquisite tits!* he felt ashamed to think, (but not *that* ashamed). He figured that if he hadn't grown up by now, little chance existed that he ever would. The reason she'd bent over was simply to pick up a rock, which she threw ten yards into the swamp.

No "plip" or splash followed, only a flat sort of "thunk."

"Sounds dry as a bone," said the Writer, "and all that fog looks....weird."

"Yeah, it's just laying flat, and I've never seen fog that color. I don't even know what to compare it to."

Yes, the color or hue of the swamp fog defied comparison to anything on the colorimetric scale: a meld of mud-brown, rot-green, and a sickly purplish blue? Something like that. The more intently the Writer looked at it, the more he fancied vague wriggling shapes moving beneath its indeterminate murk, but this he had to attribute to mere suggestion. He felt partly inclined to mention this but the thought was interrupted by a bizarre kind of *flup-flup-flupping* sound.

Both Charity and the Writer turned at once.

Something beyond comparison seemed to be, well, flupping

itself down the incline along the abbey structure. All the two spectators could do was squint.

flup-flup-flup

At each *flup,* the object seemed to squirm and then flip another foot down the incline, each movement raising a cloud of dust.

The Writer was getting tired of weird shit, and he didn't even bother uttering *What the hell is that?* or something similar. "It" had now progressed to the bottom of the incline at the rear basement wall, and Charity and the Writer could only walk up and stare down at it.

Of course, the reader already knows that this ridiculous flesh-blob was the remnants of one Michael Ling from Californ-eye-aye. Not only boneless, now, but turned *inside-out.* How it hung together in this state was anybody's guess—mesentery and other connective tissues possibly. Nevertheless, it was a quivering mass of veins, nerves, arteries, organs, and Lord knew what else. Two floating eyeballs could be seen, and possibly a prolapsed mouth, while near that a tongue wiggled.

"I...hate to say it," the Writer began, "but I'm pretty sure this is a human being–"

"Without bones."

"Yes."

"And...all messed up, like it's been turned inside-out, maybe?"

"Yes."

"Which is impossible but of course we've already seen a number of things that are impossible." He looked down at the sack of flesh. "Sorry, but I don't think there's anything we can do for you."

The mass jiggled as if in some mode of response slack, and the constituents of that prolapsed mouth managed to generate some sounds of objection, but reproducing them as written words would be useless and futile.

Wincing at the sight, the Writer gruffed, "Let's move on."

"You mean you wanna leave it like that?" Charity raised her voice. "Shouldn't it be shot, and put it out of its misery?"

The Writer offered her the pistol. "Be my guest."

Charity stared, raised her brows, and said, "Yeah, fuck it. Let's go."

The innardy pile of flesh quivered, squirmed, and squealed. Poor Michael Ling!

Our pair of explorers needed only to walk a few more steps up the incline next to the abbey before–as you no doubt also recall–their next surprise. They both stopped cold, staring down at the dead bodies of two very big, very obese men in overalls, whose heads, somehow, had been squashed together into a great chunky pulp.

"Oh, my," Charity muttered.

"I second that," said the Writer. "And unless I'm mistaken these are two of the Larkins brothers. There are four all told–quadruplets. They're the town tough guys but it looks to me that they ran into someone a *lot* tougher."

"This time," Charity said, "I think for sure it was the Bighead." She pointed down to another large bare footprint, only this was considerably smaller than the print near the torso.

The Writer just kept staring, not so much at any particular *thing*, but at the abstraction. "Okay. What have we got? We've got a dry lake full of funky fog sitting behind an absurd pre-revolutionary abbey. We've got a person with no bones who's evidently been turned inside-out, and we've got a dismembered, decapitated woman with white clay for flesh, black eyeballs, a long pink snake for a tongue, and no nipples or vagina. We've got a set of footprints that are probably the Bighead's and we've got another set of footprints that are even bigger. Oh, and we've also got two fat redneck quadruplet brothers with their skulls crushed together." He looked blankly at Charity. "Does that about sum things up?"

"No," she blurted. "We've also got *that...*"

She was pointing behind them, back toward the fog-swell of the lake. Fifty or so yards from the shore, two women were wading knee-deep in the fog–two women in black cloaks and hoods. In a few moments they stopped, seemed to attend to something, and disappeared.

* * * *

"Damn it, George! I *hate* it when you do that!" Ranger Laura Eastman yelled with something very close to disdain in her voice.

She sat spread-legged on the kiosk bench, her boots, panties, and ranger slacks fully removed, and she'd been performing on her partner's penis some preliminary fellatio in order to "gear him up" for some good ole rough and tumble intercourse. However, the process did not go as she'd hoped.

Ranger George Gemser stood a bit sheepishly before her. His ranger pants weren't off but instead bunched at his ankles, and what he'd done to trigger Laura's ire was–

"I thought you wanted to *fuck*, George!" she barked. "Shit, your dick wasn't even in my mouth ten seconds and then you pull it out and spew that shit all over my fuckin' shirt!"

This was more than plain. George had spooged her up but good, launching veritable *ropes* of semen across Laura's cute tan ranger tunic. It looked more like a mishap with a bottle of Elmer's glue. "Shit, I gotta wipe this stuff off now!" she bellyached. "Gimme a Kleenex!"

George shrugged. "Ain't got one."

"Useless!" and then she reached back to push her jet-black, shining, perfectly straight hair off her shoulder. "Oh, you prick! You got it in my hair too!"

George chuckled. "It'll wash out." He grabbed his now thoroughly deflated penis and squeezed it. "Hey, Laura! Look!"

Outraged, Laura watched as another viscid line of sperm oozed out of his dick, where it hung dangling like a piece of wet spaghetti.

She winced. "That's great, George. That's just what I want to see. I was kind of hoping to get laid today—you know, have an *orgasm?* Instead, *you* get to have one and I get nothing except your load on my shirt."

But, lo, Laura had not succeeded in securing his attention. Instead, he stood there, looking down with his hands on his hips, and apparently he was flexing some arcane pelvic muscle, the action of which made his flaccid penis jiggle up and down quite comically. When that wet piece of "spaghetti" flipped, George grinned at her. "Pretty cool, huh? How's that for talent?"

Laura could only frown back at him. *Must be my karma, I guess. I'll just have to break out the rabbit later. George is as useless as a glass hammer...* She resigned to the day and its disappointments, then began to put her pants back on.

Just then, however, George—still with his pants down at his ankles, remember—began to talk very falteringly, ""Um, um, um, Laura? You're, uh, gonna find this, um, hard to believe but-but...there's a nutty-looking woman in a black cape and sunglasses standing right behind you."

Laura didn't even bother turning around to look. She was about to hurl an appropriate remark back to him but suddenly she froze, her eyes shot wide, and she said, "George, there's a nutty-looking woman in a black cape and sunglasses standing right behind *you!*" and the nutty-looking woman in black behind Laura grabbed Laura's mane of jet-black hair, hoisted her up and—

psssssssssssssssssst!

—something almost too fast for the naked eye shot out of the woman's red-lipped mouth, touched Laura's neck, and then retracted.

-hello!-

Even half a second after this strange occurrence, Laura remained in no shape to respond to the bizarre greeting. Because in that half a second, all of her bones utterly dissolved and she was a dismayed sack of flesh oozing down the kiosk bench to the wood floor. Her only eventual vocal response was little more than a "blub-blug-glub!"

-I love making their bones go away!- said the black-clad woman. *-the new reagent works so much better through the spicule!-*

Meanwhile, the other woman in black had already dispatched poor George, who now sat ludicrously spread-legged with his pants still at his ankles and limp penis dangling.

-I'm tired of deboning them,- said the second woman in black. *-i only used the paralytic on this one.-*

-look at his penis!-

-I know! it's a funny-looking organ, isn't it?-

-it sure is! but what are you going to do with him?-

-something more fun. watch!-

By now, the reader is getting it. These women in black are aliens and their tongues are more like chameleon tongues: a long pink stretchy thing (called a ballistic hyoglossus process, if you're interested) that shoots out of their mouths at sixty mph and snags prey with a sticky pad at the end. However, in this case, there was no sticky pad but instead a "spicule" or sharp barb which injects a variety of organic reagents, catalysts, and reactants into the victim.

The full back story of these women is not necessary here (read Edward Lee's novel *Coven,* if you feel so inclined) but I will say that it had been close to thirty years since they'd last ventured to this interesting but preposterous planet called Earth. The women themselves were organically manufactured by an alien entity known as a Supremate, but we needn't go into this in detail. Here it is in brief summation, most of which you've already deduced. Extraterrestrials had landed yet again near Luntville, West Virginia, for some sinister purpose not yet disclosed.

The woman who paralyzed George was now in the process of exercising her creativity, you might say. The upside-down cross around her neck dangled as she bent over. She grinned, then opened a mouth full of sharp teeth (but don't worry, there's none of that vampire nonsense here) and from that mouth emerged that long pink tongue aka ballistic hyoglossus process, but not in a half-second snap—this time it was very slow, like a cobra arising from its basket at the sound of flutes. The tongue hovered, wavered before George's slack face, and then the tip eased forward into the ranger's mouth and began to slide down his throat.

Down, down, and down it went, while poor George Gemser could only could only sit there due to his otherworldly paralysis. Both women in black watched eagerly. The tongue seemed to be rummaging through George's innards, and in quite a monumental display...

The end of that ten-foot-plus alien tongue slid right out of George's peehole and then corkscrewed in a spectacular finish.

-see what I mean?- said the woman to her cohort, and then she giggled in an appropriately high-pitched flutter.

-wow, you're right! i wonder what other fun things we can do to these people?-

* * * *

Factory smokestacks could be seen for miles, pumping billows of murky yellow gunk into the scarlet sky. Before this panorama of factories sprawled some incalculable megalopolis of leaning black and gray buildings, drab tenements, and spiring churchlike edifices that shared no kinship with churches in the Living World.

One of these buildings boasted a sign: ESOTERIC ORDER OF DAGON, while another, much glitzier with silver mullioned windows of the lancet shape, a crocketed tower on whose point rested a nun impaled from groin to mouth, and a blood-splotched sign reading the CATHEDRAL OF THE CORRUPT INCEPTION. Evidently services had just ended, because all manner of demons, ghouls, imps, and humans (many surgically or hexgenically modified) poured from the cathedral's great double-doored entrance before a burst of cacodemoniacal organ music.

Meanwhile, the street just beyond the church was busy with traffic: steam-cars driven by vampires, zombified things like mules hauling great lopsided wagons of hacked body parts. One wagon was full of nothing but feet, the next hands, the next thighs, like that; but the last wagon was filled to the top with nothing more or less than severed male genitals, at least a thousand of them.

This was the scene that Dawn and Snowie were both peering at on the drone controller's view screen, and the looks on their faces projected expressions that most would find appropriate. "Aw, fuck!" Snowie said. "A wagon full of dicks!"

"Yeah, and look what's coming down the street now," Dawn said of a steam truck driven by a man with a vagina for a face and hauling a tanker in the back as one would expect to see on gasoline trucks, only this tanker read VOMIT RECYCLER.

Next came a break in traffic (the traffic light changed to green, which meant stop) and Dawn and Snowie could see a store on the corner with a flashing neon sign that read PREGNANT TORSOS R US! and in the front window were displayed several: naked female torsos with bloated bellies and big milk-swollen breasts—no arms, no legs, no heads, just that. It needs to be added, though, that these torsos were still alive, for their stumps roved and their bellies quivered. Several demonic customers inside were seen squeezing the breasts of some of the torsos as housewives squeeze melons in the grocery store. Other macabre patrons were caressing the distended bellies.

"Hell is even more fucked up than I thought," Dawn said.

"Yeah, just drive the drone away from there," Snowie said, wincing. "Are you sure you're even going the right way?"

"Yeah. We stayed on the same road after turning out of the

basement entrance. Look, there's the statue of the Japanese guy."

Sure enough, there was the grimy metal statue of Minister Tojo, which had been erected here on December 23, 1948, six minutes after he'd been hanged for war crimes. Dawn veered the drone around it, then followed the row of snot-gourd trees until that familiar iron fence became visible, the fence with a crest that announced LE DIABLE MANIORE.

Manse Lucifer.

"Do you really think the Devil lives there?" Snowie asked, and unceremoniously scratched her crotch.

"Who else would live in a giant mansion made of tens of thousands of severed human heads that are all still alive?" Dawn slowed the drone as the building grew closer. "I just hope I can remember where we saw Case climbing the wall. I'm sure he's gotten in by now."

"Yeah, and maybe he's gotten killed by now too! What's that thing in the fuckin' window there?" Snowie wailed.

The drone hovered before an ornate hexagonal window surrounded by smirking heads, and beyond its glass panes could be seen something like a man-shaped slab of grey meat, six feet tall. Its head was like a wedge with a flat face, eyes like chisel slits, and a gash for a mouth showing nail-like fangs. Its hands were fat-tined rakes with black talons a foot long, and its skin glistened brownish-gray, something like slug skin.

Dawn gulped. "Whatever that thing is, it's one tough customer, and I gotta feeling there's plenty of them in there."

"Maybe the Devil's security guards," Snowie guessed. "Giant Gumby dolls with fangs."

"Case won't stand a chance against it, even with his gun. But we gotta go in anyway and try to find him." Dawn eased the controller's joystick forward and traversed the camera back and forth, surveying for a suitable aperture within the massive wall of living, blinking heads, which jabbered, yelled, and screamed as the drone moved along. "Look! There!" she exclaimed when a balcony was revealed. "And the french doors are open! Now we're in luck…"

The drone pushed through the gap between curtains made of skin dotted with infected sores. "Fuck," Snowie muttered. "More heads!"

It was now apparent that more than just the mansion's outer walls were made of human heads. Indeed, inside was a long vanishing point of ballrooms, state rooms, dining halls, galleries, etc., all of whose walls, ceilings, and floors were constructed with living human heads.

"Shit," Dawn observed. "It's not tens of thousands or even hundreds of thousands of heads that built this place. It must be millions."

Snowie was getting dizzy looking at this enormity of heads, even on the little view screen. "Dang, the Devil shore is one really sick dude! Must really hate humans, too!"

Dawn buzzed the drone through the first ballroom and into a circular gallery centered by a great fountain with a statue of a voluptuous, big-titted succubus standing on a pedestal in the middle. The statue stood with its hands on curvaceous hips and lewdly spread-legged. From a hole between the effigy's legs gushed the "water" of the fountain: lumpy menstrual blood.

"That's charming," Dawn said. "And what's this room here?" She took the drone into a long, head-walled parlor wherein stood a solitary wooden door with a rounded top. Mounted in the middle of it was an iron spike.

Dawn and Snowie both traded uneasy glances. "That looks an awful lot like the doors here in Crafter's basement, including the opened one leading to Hell," Snowie said.

"Yeah, fuck it. Let's move on." The drone backed out of the room and headed to the next, which contained an item with a very familiar configuration.

Snowie was squinting. "Hey, does that look like a–?"

"–a toilet," said Dawn. "But-but-but–"

It was made with human heads.

That's right, human heads cemented together comprised the bowl; the faces, naturally, were all turned to form the *inside* of the bowl. Another row of heads, all face up, sufficed for the seat.

"It's the Devil's toilet!" Dawn exclaimed.

"Nasty! And why is that one head sitting there loose?"

Yes, a separate head sat sideways on a raised pedestal next to the toilet. Like most of them, it was a female head, with blonde tousles for hair and pretty green eyes. Now, remember, this woman's head was *alive,* and another detail worth mentioning was the fact that there were brown smears running from the head's chin to forehead. Even less-than-razor-sharp intellects such as those of Snowie and Dawn could quickly realize the purpose of this particular head placed right next to the Devil's toilet.

"She's his toilet paper!" they cried together.

"Bleck!" uttered the severed head. For a moment the face looked like that woman...what was her name? Anna Nicole something? But...no, that couldn't be right. It was probably just some other woman who looked like her.

Dawn didn't dawdle pulling the drone out of the bathroom. She veered the machine down another head-lined hallway. Then it buzzed into another room which appeared to be a kitchen where purple-skinned trolls were preparing what was evidently Satan's next meal—not Peking Duck but Peking Human. Slabs of meat with the skin still on were lowered by wires into kiln-like ovens, and here the slabs were meticulously roasted while all fat melted out from between the flesh and skin until the skin became delectably crispy.

As Dawn traversed the camera to see where the meat slabs had come from, she and Snowie both said in unison, "Holy shit..."

A fresh corpse hung from a meat hook, already relieved of its arms and legs. A piggish-faced troll busied itself by adroitly eviscerating what was left of the corpse, while another troll hobbled forward with a tool that looked like an over-large pair of branch-cutters and asked, "Should I start the brain pudding now?"

"Yeah," answered the first, winnowing out the liver from the rest of the innards. "And put a little aside for us."

The second troll nodded, then raised its great dual-handled implement, splaying two crescent-shaped blades to fit under the corpse's neck, but of course by then Dawn and Snowie had already recognized the face of the victim on the hook.

It was Case.

"Oh, man," moaned Dawn, "that poor fucker. And I was kind of hot for him."

"Me, too," said Snowie, "Fuck! He never shoulda gone in there!"

"At least his soul is in Heaven now."

Snowie looked crookedly at her. "Ya think there really *is* a Heaven?"

Dawn frowned. "How can you *not*? We're watching a *live stream* of *Hell*, you dingbat!"

Snowie stared into space. "Oh, yeah..."

The drone pulled out of the kitchen and continued to explore. Dawn was hoping to get a glimpse of the Devil himself, but she had to admit, the walls of severed heads notwithstanding, Lucifer's house wasn't exactly a happenin' place. A few bats flew across the next hall–bats with vaguely human faces–and in the next they passed a statue of someone that seemed to be *made* of feces, but that was about it. Evidently, modern art wasn't quite the same thing in Hell.

Where was Jackson Pollock when you needed him?

"What's this down here?" Dawn said. "It looks like some kind of a chapel."

"Chapel? What kinda chapel would they have in Hell?"

"I'm gonna check it out. Nothing else to do here now that we know Case is dead."

Two pillars of mirror-finished black stone formed the entry to a chapel-like alcove lit dimly with some indescribable light. The walls within were not constructed of human heads but of a jet-black substance that seemed luminous. Dawn and Snowie, even only able to see via the drone-controller's screen, were captivated by its blackish luminescence.

"Hey," Dawn said. "Look at this..." She turned the camera to the right side of the cove, and there, mounted on the wall, stood a black door with a rounded top and a metal spike sticking out of it.

"It's another door like the ones in this here basement, and in that parlor down the hall!" Snowie exclaimed.

"Yeah, and what's this shit over *here?*" Dawn turned the cam to the other side wall where there stood an altar of black stone, and on it, a naked headless woman lay with her legs widely parted while a naked headless man was humping her hell for leather.

"Gross!" Snowie said. "Hell really is one fucked up place. Good thing Paulie ain't here; he'd make us film it for his most perverted clients."

Dawn was about to add something to the remark but went into a long pause instead, then said, "Since you mentioned Paulie...have you heard from him or Augie?"

"Nope."

"Neither have I, and that's kind of odd, isn't it? It's been a while since those sick fucks have bothered us. Better check our phones." Dawn pressed the HOVER button on the controller, and they both pulled out their phones. "Shit," she griped. "Mine's dead! I must've forgotten to charge it!"

Snowie brought a hand to her mouth and moaned, "Oh no no no no no..."

"Your phone's dead too?"

"No! Damn thing musta got switched to silent! There's like a dozen voicemails from them!"

Dawn began to shake in sheer terror. "Luh-luh listen to the most recent one..."

Snowie's hands shook in the same sheer terror as she dialed, put the phone to her ear, and listened. Then she gulped and hung up.

"Well?" Dawn asked.

"Fuuuuuuck. It was Augie. He says he's gonna fuck us up good for ducking his calls. Says when he finds us, he's gonna blow torch our assholes, then our pussies, then our faces!"

The two women stared at each other for a full minute. "What are we gonna do?" Dawn said. "We can never go home again!"

"At least there's no way he can find us out here."

Dawn looked even more fretful. "I dunno; all smart phones have a locator chip in them. If you know what you're doing you can activate it and find out where it is. But there's no way those olive-oil greaseball morons would know about that."

Snowie let out a relieved breath. "Yeah, those goombahs are dopes."

"Still, we should probably ditch or destroy them first, just in case."

Isn't it curious how the most potent of coincidences always seem to pile up in works of fiction, especially in a way that utterly contradicts the certainties of the characters? Because at that self-same moment, a door slammed upstairs, footsteps tramped down the steps and, of course—

Dawn and Snowie both screamed.

—Paulie Vinchetti appeared.

He looked a mess: hair sticking up, shirt tail out, sports jacket crumpled, and crazy-eyed as ever. His receding forehead shined from sweat, and in one hand he waved a pistol.

Both girls cowered on their knees in the corner. "Please, Mr. Vinchetti!" Dawn pleaded. "Don't kill us! We weren't ducking your calls—our phones weren't charged!"

"Yeah, Mr. Vinchetti!" Snowie blubbered. "Please don't blow-torch our cooters!"

But at that point one thing became clear: it wasn't bloodlust that accounted for Paulie's maniacal look, it was fear. "Naw, naw, forget about all that shit! You girls gotta help me! There's some fucked up shit going on outside!" The degree of Paulie's upset was made even more plain: he was crying. "Augie's dead, see? These whacked-out women in black cloaks and sunglasses did something to him and made—and made—aw, fuck!—they made his bones melt! And they was both wearin' these upside-down crosses. Like what them devil-worshipers wear!"

Dawn and Snowie both traded glances that might easily be labeled "appropriate."

Paulie was jittering, he was so scared. "My car's fucked up, too. I'm beggin' youse girls, ya gotta get me away from here. I'll pay ya, I'll do anything. Saw a white Chevy out the end of the road, but it ain't got no keys in it. Do either'a you's have 'em?"

Dawn's brows rose. "I have the keys right here." She pulled them out and showed him.

Paulie nearly wilted in relief. He leaned against the granite altar where the grimoire and other books sat, and he let out a long sigh. "God bless ya!" Then he pulled out a handkerchief and patted the sweat off his brow. Only in this interim did he notice the oddities present in the basement. "What's them doors there? And what's with the dead guy?" This last reference, of course, was the body of Pastor Tommy, who'd been impaled on one of the doors.

"It's a long story, Mr. Vinchetti," Dawn said.

As Paulie pointed to the door on the end which, as we all know, was wide open, there was one other thing he did.

He set his pistol down.

Dawn shot Snowie a quick wink, and Snowie cut the slightest of smiles.

"Oh, that?" Dawn said, walking over to Paulie. "It just goes to another part of the basement. The Writer thought there were valuable books down there, but there was nothing. Let's forget about this dump and get you out of here, Mr. Vinchetti."

"Yeah, good idea. The fuck I care about a stiff and some open door?" Paulie said. "Let's split, and I mean now. Fuck knows where them devil chicks are."

When Paulie was about to pick his gun back up, Dawn grabbed his arm with one hand and his hair with the other, while Snowie grabbed his collar, and they both began to shove him backward.

Paulie had just time to yell, "Why you cut-throat fuckin' fuck-buckets! I'm gonna fuck you both up so bad–" and then–

SLAM!

–he was slammed back-first against another of the doors aka "traversion bridles." The iron spike in the middle of the door did a perfect job of puncturing Paulie's upper body; in fact it may have penetrated the aorta itself, for quite a shower of blood began to pump out on the stone floor.

"Wow! Wud'ja lookit that!" Snowie yelled in glee.

Paulie shivered on the spike, mouthing some such as "Gonna have my boys knock up the both'a you'se, then steam-roll ya..."

"Only thing you're gonna do," Dawn assured, "is fuckin' die slow." The shower of blood was already abating. She grabbed her accomplice. "Snowie, pull his pants down, quick!"

"Pull his–why?"

"Just do it, before he croaks!"

Snowie did as asked, and yanked down the mafioso's Prussian gray Gucci slacks, to theatrically reveal his bunched, withered junk, so small it was nearly overwhelmed by the plot of pubic hair. All that showed of his dick was the meager corona, like one of those button mushrooms you find in your Triple Delight at Chinese take-out places.

Dawn wasted no time positioning herself, and with the proficiency of a place-kicker, she advanced on her target and– one, two, three–

FWAP!

–kicked Paulie's balls *hard* with the bridge of her artificial foot.

Paulie, still infinitesimally alive, gave a groan like a just-gelded bull.

"Fuck, I always wanted to do that!" she celebrated. "All the times this scumbag made me *suck* his dick, now I can *kick* it," and then–

FWAP!

–she kicked it again, this time so hard that the whites of Paulie's eyes seemed to hemorrhage in a split second.

"Yeah?" Snowie intoned. "Well, watch this!"

It should go without saying that this was not the first time Snowie had willingly lowered herself to her knees before a man's genitals; even to say that it had been the *thousandth* time would, I'm afraid, have fallen short of the mark. Nevertheless, there she knelt, before a barely alive Paulie and his grievously retracted penis. She fished around with his scrotum, managed to isolate a single testicle, and then she "ringed" it with her thumb and forefinger, exerting sufficient pressure until that testicle extruded forward, tight against the skin.

"Saw one'a the Larkins brothers do this to a drug-dealer they up'n catched at Dean's Corners," and then Snowie opened her mouth, inched her head slowly forward, then gently placed the testicle between her upper and lower front teeth, and then in one great surge of mandibular action–

–*click!*

–divided that pulsing, veiny goombah testicle into near perfect halves.

Now, remember, Paulie had the best of both feet in the grave already, but Snowie's deft use of her incisors did manage to succeed in producing in Paulie's nervous system a good solid kick of reactive agony.

"*That* gave the motherfucker something to remember us by!" Dawn shouted with glee.

"Aw, fuck," Snowie moaned. "That felt *sooo* good..."

Now the two girls embraced and began to jump around in a maniacal and celebratory dance. "Just think of it!" Dawn said. "No more sucking his dick, no more swallowing his cum, no more taking it up the ass, and, and, and–"

"No more corpse-porn!" Snowie shrieked.

"What a great day!"

Indeed it was!

"What was all that crazy shit he was talking? Augie's dead? And—"

"Yeah," Snowie jumped in, "And some shit about chicks in cloaks, and Augie's bones melting? I *knew* them guys took drugs. What a couple idjits!"

But the topic at hand soon dwindled for Dawn. What with Paulie and Augie both being dead, Dawn's fuse was officially *lit*, and she pushed up Snowie's shirt and in a second had those big farm-girl tits in her hands.

"Fuck this shit," she resolved. "I gotta eat me some box!"

She grabbed Snowie just under the hips, plopped her butt down on the stone altar, and, without missing a beat, hauled Snowie's jeans right off her legs in one perfectly synchronized action, flopped Snowie's knees over her shoulders and went to town. She pushed her face right into her companion's big kinky yellow-white bush, and burrowed deep down into the special parts, tongue fishing for that wonderful, malty flesh.

And you can bet your ass that Snowie was getting *into* it: ass clenching, nipples erecting, vagina quivering, and her tongue hanging out like a St Bernard. Just when she was about to let 'er rip with a very vocal orgasm, the reverie was interrupted by the strangest noise: a low, creaking sound. The sound was so distinctive, unpleasant, and distracting that all hope of having a raucous orgasm disintegrated at once.

"What the *fuck* was that?" Snowie asked.

Dawn disconnected her face from her friend's gaping crotch and walked over to where Paulie's impaled body hung. She knew *exactly* what the sound was. Snowie—still pantsless, remember—followed her over.

"Death-rattle," Dawn said, ever familiar with that emphatic sound which escorted a person's final living moment.

Paulie just hung there, limp dick out, the end of his penis dribbling urine.

"Can't believe the fuck is really dead!" Snowie blinked, looked at Paulie's corpse, at Pastor Tommy's corpse, and then at the one open door at the end of the row. "But wait a minute. I thunk—"

"*Thought*, Snowie. Not *thunk.*"

"Whatever! I thought every time someone got nailed to one'a these here doors, another one was s'posd'ta open..."

Dawn jumped into the middle of Snowie's observation. "You're right. That's what the Writer said. He called these doors 'traversion bridles' or something. One of them should've opened when Paulie died..." She looked closely at Paulie's body hanging on the door. "Unless maybe he's not quite dead yet."

Just as she voiced that speculation, a few more of those creepy death-rattle clicks issued from Paulie's mouth. Then two more, then one more, then a pause, and then a final click, and—

WHAM!

The second to last traversion door slammed open. A great howling was heard, like a gale from beyond, like a tornado very far away. There was a moment of stillness, then in an instant, some kind of reverse pressure *cracked* into the basement. Both Snowie and Dawn's hair stood straight out as they began to feel the pull. Snowie's pants, still on the floor, were the first things to be drawn into newly opened doorway. Then several books got sucked in, and a few empty beer bottles.

Dawn felt the force pulling on her own body as it gained strength, so she ducked behind the stone altar. "Snowie!" she yelled. "Grab onto something!"

"What?" Snowie shouted over the roar.

Dawn edged her head just above the altar-top in just enough time to see Snowie get picked off her feet and whisked bare-assed through the doorway.

* * * *

"You saw that, right?" asked the Writer.

Charity sighed. "You mean, did I see two women in black cloaks just disappear in the middle of the swamp? Yes, I think I did."

The sun was sinking fast now, tinting the crannies of the surrounding forest with darkness, and along with this, the oddity of the swamp fog became more apparent: ever so faintly, it was beginning to glow as if from some inner greenish luminosity.

"Should we...check it out?" said the Writer with very little enthusiasm.

"I'm ready if you are," Charity said, grabbed his hand, headed for the swamp.

Of course, the Writer wasn't at all sure that he was ready for any such thing, yet he followed her just the same. They went back down the hill, crossed the shore, and marched right into the body of the fog. This swamp or lake or whatever it was, had indeed been fully drained long ago; even by the time the Writer and Charity had gone thirty yards into it, there was no trace of water, nor wetness. Another thing: the fog felt vaguely warm.

"Now," observed the Writer, "we both saw those two women disappear right about here, didn't we?"

"This looks about right..."

"So...it must've been a trick of light, or–" He pinched his chin. "Or..."

"Or they're aliens," Charity said, "like we considered."

"I agree," the Writer said with some anguish, "but it's just not so easy for me to believe that, even with all the other wild stuff we've seen." As he said that, he stepped back, but that step was impeded immediately. It felt as though he'd backed up against a wall, but when he looked...there *was* no wall. There was nothing there.

"What?" Charity asked.

He put his hand up, pressing it forward until its progress was halted by some obstruction he couldn't see. Then he grabbed Charity's hand and put it in the same place.

"What the hell is that!" she half-shrieked. "There's something there–"

"Yeah, like a wall."

"–but it's invisible!"

The Writer side-stepped to the left, running his hand against the invisible solid object. He proceeded only about four feet before he came to the object's edge. His fingers curled around that edge to find another invisible flat surface, and this extended about four more feet. At the end of this little exploratory venture, he discovered that the invisible object must be about four feet square, but when he reached up as high as his own physical height would permit, he could not discover how high this inexplicable object rose.

Charity was feeling around it too. "What on Earth can this be?"

Yeah, pondered the Writer. *What ON EARTH?* It seemed, now, that the next step in solving this mystery–even if "aliens" *were* afoot–could not be deduced. But surprises often occurred at opportune times, and right then the Writer's cell phone rang.

He had a strong feeling who the caller might be even before he looked at the phone and saw UNKNOWN NUMBER on the screen.

He answered it, "You again."

"That's right, bro," his doppelganger replied. "Once again, I must avail myself to keep your dumb ass headed in the right direction. You really are dumber than a box of rocks."

"Thanks," was all the Writer could think to say back.

"I guess you really are getting too old. I mean, how unobservant can you be?"

Now the Writer bellowed, "How can I observe something that's fuckin' INVISIBLE?"

Crunching sounds could be heard over the line. The

doppelganger was eating as he commenced with the conversation. "All right. I guess I'll have to take you by your little hand and walk you through, like I always do. Now, you've pretty much figured out that those women in the black cloaks are aliens, right?"

"Well, since you're saying so, then I guess they are, because you're so much smarter than me."

"Ah. Now we're getting somewhere. And what did you do after you and the woman with the giant pussy found the alien body parts?"

"Her name is Charity! And...what do you mean? Yeah, we found a dismembered woman, arms and legs with no bones or muscles, the head squashed, a long red tongue–oh–and the torso with a giant footprint in it."

"Yeah, yeah," said the doppelganger, impatient. "But what else? *You* did something, didn't you?"

The Writer squinted, pressing his memory. In the meantime, his doppelganger continued eating food and smacking his lips. *That's so fuckin' rude!* But as for whatever else the Writer supposedly *did* upon discovering the body parts with Charity, he could not conceive of a guess.

The doppelganger sighed. "You're *so* dense; I can't believe we're both the same person, sort of. Let me ask you something. Did you by chance happen to pick anything up *off the ground?*"

The Writer blinked. "Oh, yeah, I did. But it was just a pendant of an upside-down cross and a pair of sunglasses. No big deal."

"No big deal? What does any other person in the world do when they find a pair of sunglasses?"

Now the Writer was getting rankled. "How would I know? I picked 'em up and put 'em in my bag! I didn't give much thought to it! I thought maybe I might have a use for them later. So what?"

The doppelganger took another bite out of whatever he was

eating, and said, "Did it ever occur to you to maybe, like, try them on?" Then he hung up.

Oh, for shit's sake! But maybe the doppelganger had a bit of a point. Maybe it *was* a natural reaction when one finds a pair of sunglasses to try them on and see if they like them.

Therefore, the Writer reached into his plastic bag, fetched the black sunglasses, and put them on.

He looked around, then he looked upward. Then he lost consciousness and collapsed.

* * * *

Now, if you'll recall, in the transition before last, another basement door swung open at the moment of Paulie Vinchetti's death, and a brief "vacuum" ensued, which sucked poor Snowie through the doorway (with no pants on, remember), and in the wink of an eye, she was gone.

Dawn, still watching from around the stone altar, thought, *Holy fuck!* and shortly thereafter, that initial vacuum action ceased which allowed her to stand upright and run to the door.

"Snowie!" she yelled. "Fuck! Come back!"

But there was no response, no visible sign of Snowie, and in fact nothing visible at all in the black tunnel that twisted away from the newly opened doorway.

"Fuck fuck!" Dawn uttered. "Fuck fuck fuck! Snowie just got sucked into Hell!"

For a moment, Dawn resolved to go in after her...but that moment lapsed utterly. Did this door lead to the same area of Hell that the first door did? *I'll bring the drone back from the first door and send it into this one!*

It seemed a good idea. (Of course, a better one would be to send in the second drone she'd bought, on a fully charged battery but, honestly, in all the commotion, this idea did not occur to her.) She grabbed the controller for the first drone, was about to press the RETURN button, but froze when she looked at the screen.

There was the drone where she'd last seen it, still hovering in mid-air before the spiked black door in the alcove. The walls of this alcove, as noted before, were jet-black and weirdly luminous, and if anything, that luminescence seemed more vibrant now. But there was one other, bigger, difference.

The spiked door, which had been shut previously, now stood open.

Dawn realized, *The minute Paulie died, the door in this basement opened, but that door must've opened too...* Could Paulie's death actually have triggered *both* doors to open? *This is just getting too fucked up,* Dawn thought. She didn't know what to do. Snowie was in Hell (with no pants on), but here was *this* door, wide open, and already *in* Hell. Dawn was half-tempted to send *this* drone into *this* door, but...

No, I've got to go after Snowie, she realized. *It's the only decent thing to do.*

Ah, but how unsearchable are the mechanics of fate! Just as Dawn was about push the button to return the drone—

WHOOSH!

—the same sort of vacuum action that had sucked Snowie into the basement doorway gusted once and sucked the drone into the black alcove's doorway.

It was impossible not to watch the controller screen as the drone whisked down an indeterminate black corridor, swaying this way and that, with only the most minuscule dot of greenish-white light visible at the corridor's terminus. This looked quite a bit different from the other corridor that had led to the road in Hell on which they'd found Manse Lucifer.

Eventually, the drone was ejected into some sort of room with walls of shimmering white-green light. Here Dawn commanded the drone to stop and hover. Seemingly embedded in the glowing center wall was a familiar symbol, that of an upside-down cross, but in radiant scarlet, which blurred like a fluorescent tube, and sticking out of the cross's absolute midpoint was a pointed black spike.

The same weirdo shit as here in Crafter's basement, just different colors, Dawn realized.

But this place didn't look at all like a street in Hell.

She drove the drone through one of the four doorway-like portals in this little lit anteroom, and what she entered was a perfectly straight jet-black corridor. But there was something odd about the "blackness"; perhaps it came with the screen's reproduction, but it struck Dawn that the utter blackness of the walls was emanating some sort of colorless light which didn't interfere with the blackness.

What is this fucked up place? Is it some other part of Hell?

The corridor appeared endless and perfectly straight and coruscating with a light that could only be called lightless. Eventually she noticed that every twenty or so feet, to the left and right, there were other square black doorways, but when she traversed the camera to look in, nothing was evident, just another undefinable depth of radiant black.

Whatever this shit is, Dawn decided, *it's not doing me any good being here, so...* Again she was about to press the RETURN button when—

—she heard a scream.

Dawn's first instinctive impulse was to pull the drone back now, but the thing was—

Fuck, that voice sounds familiar...

When she pointed the drone cam into the next doorway, she all but dropped the controller.

A pale figure lay crumpled in the next cove, a *human* figure. On top of that, the figure was that of a woman, and this fact was easily discerned because she wore no pants and lay there on her back with her legs spread.

I know that hairy pussy anywhere! Dawn thought. It was Snowie.

But how could this be? Snowie had been sucked into the door in Crafter's basement, but Dawn had driven the drone through the black door in Manse Lucifer. Both doors, or traversion bridles, had led to the same place!

And I don't even know what this place is, Dawn said to herself. But there Snowie lay on the floor, unconscious. Dawn could tell she wasn't dead because the big tits stuffed under her shirt rose and fell. On the screen, Dawn noticed something odd as well: in Snowie's hand was a pair of black sunglasses. Dawn had never seen Snowie wear sunglasses in her life, and even if she had a pair, why get them out in this dark place?

I gotta wake her up somehow, and her next idea was to slowly lower the drone over Snowie's face in hopes that the motor buzz and the force of the air from the props might have the sought-after effect.

When that didn't work, she bounced the drone repeatedly on Snowie's left boob...but with no success. But next...

She maneuvered the drone over Snowie's brazenly displayed crotch, canted it forwarded, then skidded one of the drone's propeller blades right about where the clitoris was–

"Oooow! Fuck!" Snowie yelled and came to.

She pushed herself up on her hands, vigorously shook her head, and blinked out of her stupor. Then she looked, bewildered, at the hovering drone. "That's-that's *you,* ain't it, Dawn?"

Dawn answered yes by moving the drone up and down.

"And how-how did *you* get here?"

Of course, there was no way to answer so Dawn just hovered.

"Oh, that's right–you can hear me but I can't hear you, right?"

Dawn bobbed the drone yes again.

Snowie stammered on, half hysterical. "I thought shore I'd wind up in Hell 'cos that's where the first door led to, but this *ain't* Hell. Do you know what it *is?*"

Dawn slid the drone back and forth sideways for no.

"Lemme show ya!" She picked up the sunglasses with one hand and grabbed the drone's landing legs with the other. She angled the drone upward. "I'm gonna put the sunglasses over the camera lens," Snowie said. "Then you'll see what this fuckin' place *really* is..."

Back in Crafter's basement, Dawn was barely able to keep from collapsing while staring at the screen. Once Snowie held the sunglasses over the camera lens, that previous impression of vaguely luminous black walls transfigured into an impossible vertiginous vista of glowing lines and compartments. If anything, the lines more resembled pipes, and the entire scenario more resembled blueprints or some kind of schematic of plumbing. Tiny lights of every color blinked, pulsed, and throbbed, but they were not "dots" but more like slashes which shifted in length. As for the "pipes," the ones that were closer seemed to be transparent, and in some of them—yes—things moved, things like people, walking back and forth in some endless onus. It became clear—after the initial shock— that the "pipes" were actually passageways that existed as an immense and unfathomable network. And the "people" in these passages were walking up and down, sideways, upside-down, every which way. Defying gravity. Everything Dawn looked at on the screen appeared endless.

Snowie's face slid back into view. "See what I fuckin' mean? You see the people walkin' around in those pipes? They go on for miles! And in between the pipes, you can sometimes see little *things* moving around, almost like they'se *flying.* There's all these *lights,* too—probably millions of them! You can't see where it all ends. It's a fuckin' giant *spaceship!*"

Dawn continued to stare at the controller screen while Snowie's words sunk in. A spaceship. What she was looking at was, indeed, impossible. When viewed through the filter of the sunglasses, there didn't appear to be any limit of the place's dimensions. So, spaceship was starting to sound good right now, as an explanation, even though Dawn didn't believe in spaceships. Its immensity was incalculable; it was like being lost inside an aircraft carrier, or *ten* aircraft carriers.

"And lookit this!" Snowie urged. She walked briskly down the corridor, still holding the drone by the landing struts.

"When you're goin' along these fucked-up black hallways, there's these kinda side-rooms, like what we seen on the screen in the Devil's house! With spiked doors just like in Crafter's basement!" Of course, her tits bounced and her very bare ass joggled when she trotted a bit farther. Then she stopped and turned to her right. She held the drone and sunglasses back up. "See, right here..."

What Dawn saw on the screen was an effulgent-black alcove akin to the one in Manse Lucifer, only here the glowing black walls seemed to warp what she might expect of dimensionality. There was, too, a luminous line on the rear wall in the shape of a doorway with a rounded top just like the doors in Crafter's basement and, yes, mounted in this outline's center was a very sharp black spike.

And there was one more thing worthy of mention...

A red, glowing. upside-down cross just above the outline.

What the FUCK? Dawn thought

Snowie looked right into the drone's lens and echoed her very thought. "What the *fuck,* huh? Crafter's basement gots a door what leads to Hell, but also gots a door what leads to this fuckin' spaceship! And the fuckin' spaceship has a door just like those! And there's a fuckin' upside-down cross over it, and upside-down crosses are symbols of devil worship! So don't that all mean the *aliens* in this fuckin' *spaceship* are *Satanists?*"

Dawn, as frantic as she felt, wished she could answer, because it was obvious now. *Satanic aliens... Of all the shit...* But what she had to do now was think of a way to get Snowie out of *there* and back *here.* These doors were like teleporters in a movie– *Only this ISN'T a movie!*

Maybe if I press the RETURN button, Snowie could follow the drone back through the door here that led to Manse Lucifer and then back from there to here...

Snowie let go of the drone as if she was having the same idea. It resumed hovering. Dawn pressed the RETURN button.

Which, of course, was when the battery died.

* * * *

The Writer's wobbly consciousness came back to him like a bubble rising to the surface of a pool of water. He felt an arm around his back and a hand patting, almost slapping his cheek.

"Are you all right, are you all right?" he heard an echoic and vaguely sexy voice ask.

Of course, it was Charity. *She was right next to me when I–* When he *what?*

When I put on the sunglasses and looked up!

What he had seen was this: a jet-black monolithic structure a thousand–no, *thousands*–of feet high. Its blackness was imperceptibly luminous. Perhaps an effective way to describe it would be to ask you to imagine the Empire State Building turned upside-down and standing on its antenna, but all black.

In the name of Ixion, King of the Lapiths, thought the Writer, as the jolt of the recollection knocked all the air from his lungs. "I must be out of my mind. I *couldn't* have seen what I thought I saw..."

"I saw it too, so you're not out of your mind," Charity said.

Via the way Charity was crouching over him, one splendiferous boob had half- slipped over the sundress' neckline, and the Writer had no choice but to stare at it even as he cogitated this most recent revelation. "It's a gargantuan spaceship, isn't it? I mean, an *invisible* gargantuan spaceship."

"I don't see what else it can be," Charity said. "But at least we've learned one secret. The sunglasses that those women in black wear are more than just sunglasses, and I'll bet they have many other properties too, especially when you consider the technology involved here. We've got to find a way inside."

"No, we *don't*," the Writer asserted, instantly outraged. "I think it's safe to say we're already in over our heads. Fuck. We came out here looking for your brother the Bighead–who, by the way, is a genuine *monster*–and what do we find instead? Alien goth girls in black cloaks and an invisible spaceship that's so tall you can't see the end of it."

"I thought you were a writer," Charity said. "Writers are supposed to want to experience unique things and write about them."

"Not *this* writer," the Writer said. "This writer is *done* for the day. I've had enough. The only thing I wanna do now is go back to Luntville, go to the bar, and drink beer till I'm pissy drunk."

Charity ignored him. She put the sunglasses back on, then reached into the Writer's plastic bag, fished out the black pendant he'd found, and examined the area where they'd seen those two women disappear. "Just as I thought," she said. "This is more than just a satanic pendant, too." She stuck the bottom of the upside-down cross into the thin air, turned it, and there came a *click!*

Instantly, an oblong, door-sized aperture formed in midair. The Writer's mouth gaped. "So those pendants are really keys..."

"No doubt about it," Charity said. "But you have to have the sunglasses on to see the keyholes. Come on."

What else could the Writer do? He followed her into the impossible doorway.

What they'd stepped into (as you've already deduced) was a black corridor that seemed endless, while its "blackness" appeared vaguely luminous, and this corridor absolutely contradicted dimensionality as the Writer understood it.

"This is impossible," he said, but it was really an unnecessary remark–in fact, perhaps the most useless thing he'd ever said. *What HASN'T been impossible today?*

"Yeah?" Charity said. She took off the sunglasses and passed them over. "Put those on and then tell me about impossible..."

The corridor he'd just stepped into was like an oblong black tunnel, and that was about it, but with the glasses on, he almost passed out again. Now he stood in a black, glowing maze constellated with millions of blinking lights and uncountable layers or strata. Up, down, and to all sides these layers extended, until sheer distance made them disappear to his vision; everywhere he looked these layers (which clearly functioned as still more corridors or tunnels) presented endless vanishing points hovering in a three-dimensional scope of vision.

Did they extend for miles before he could no longer see them, or *hundreds* of miles? This he couldn't guess, but it was obvious that this "spaceship" existed in a fashion contrary to all known earthly physics and understandings of dimensionality. The place reminded him of the graphical visuality of that movie *Tron* (the first one, NOT the second one) with its endless black convergence point.

The Writer stared back at all this, in every direction, for another minute, then wobbled in place, said "I think I might throw up," and then–

He threw up.

"Wow," said Charity.

It was a robust upchuck, and the Writer really did urp out a sound like *RAALF!* The plume splattered on the spaceship floor with a sequent sound that echoed wetly down the corridor and back.

"Fuck," the Writer remarked. He wiped his mouth with a hand, wiped the hand on the wall, then looked down at his splay of vomit. "Sorry about that. Think they have a janitor here?"

"Seeing the real nature of this place with the aid of those glasses," Charity said, "is quite a bit to experience all at once and with no warning. I almost threw up too. On the inside, it looks much bigger than that monolith standing in the swamp. I mean, just how big is this place?"

"I don't know, and I don't want to find out," said the Writer. "Anyway, we've entered the spaceship. Great. Now let's turn right back around and go out the way we came in."

Charity sluffed off the suggestion, and continued forward. "Let's look around a little more. After all, it *is* a spaceship."

The Writer continued to follow her, finding his urge to object strangely dwindling and becoming usurped by another, more acute sensitivity.

Fuck. I'm horny as shit again. What gives?

As he walked his eyes focused hard on Charity's dynamite ass wagging beneath her sundress. An erection was burgeoning in his pants in a half second; he had to grit his teeth as his steps continued.

For pity's sake, I've already had three orgasms today, and now I'm ready for a fourth. That's not supposed to happen with guys my age...

Just ahead, however, Charity stopped and turned to her right. "Look at this," she said.

Whatever *this* was, the Writer wasn't looking at it. He was looking at the side-shot of her magnificent right boob printing against her top. The Writer squeezed his crotch–he couldn't help it. *Damn, I gotta bust another one!* he thought. But, eventually, he did take note of what she was looking at.

"What is that? A closet or something?"

"It's some kind of alcove," she said.

Yeah, he thought. *A Satanic one.*

A man-high, rectangular indentation cut into the black wall several feet deep and about six feet wide. On the rear wall stood an oblong shape with a rounded top, a bit like the bridle doors in Crafter's basement, and embossed in the middle of this was another upside-down cross.

"Can you see that cross without the sunglasses?" Charity asked.

"Yes. More evidence that we're dealing with Satanic aliens. Just more food for thought. Why would God and the Devil be reserved only for Earth if God created the entire universe and countless more habitable planets?"

"I'm not worried about that now," Charity said. "This thing here is the same shape as the doors in Crafter's basement, and I want to know what's behind it."

The Writer winced. "Just more alien shit! What do we care? Look, you wanted to see the inside of the spaceship; well, now you have. So lets go back the way we came and get out of here!"

"I'll only be a minute." Dismissing him, she raised the pendant/key. She was about to insert it into the keyhole in the panel but–

"Wait!" the Writer shouted and rushed her.

He grabbed her, spun her around, then mashed his lips against hers and stuck his tongue in her mouth. He also frantically felt up her tits, squeezed her ass, and marauded her crotch with his hand.

"What are you doing?" she asked, smirking.

"I'm just...making a desperate gesture of affection in case I never see you again." Now both hands shucked her breasts out and squeezed them alternately. He also took the liberty of grinding his groin against her thigh. "How about you jerk me off on your tit again, and I arm-fuck you?"

She nudged him away, smiling. "Maybe later. And I'm feeling it too. There's something about the atmosphere of this place that's heightening our sex-drives. We have to stay focused."

Fuck focused, he thought, and groaned when she put her breasts back in her top. His erection pounded in his pants. He sighed when she stuck the bottom of the pendant in the hole in the door-panel. A *CLUNK!* sound was heard, the doorway disappeared, and then–

You're shitting me, the Writer thought.

Snowie stumbled out of the opening, wild-eyed, boobs jiggling in her shirt, totally bereft of pants. She bumped right into the Writer, shrieked, recognized him, and shrieked again.

"Good God dang! It's you!" She hugged him in a manner that squashed her breasts again him, doing little for helping him stay focused.

"Snowie!" he yelled. "You're supposed to be with Dawn at Crafter's house, trying to lead Case back!"

"Yeah, scratch that; Case is fuckin' dead! We saw his body in the Devil's kitchen! A couple purple monsters was gettin' ready to *cook* him!"

"That's hideous," Charity remarked, "but...*how* did you get here?"

It was here that Snowie recited the long-winded details of the sequence of events that had led her into the bowels of this monolithic spaceship. Both Charity and the Writer listened attentively, especially the Writer, whose gaze flicked back and forth between Snowie's breasts in her top, and her bounteous white pubic patch, which was easily viewed since, as you know, she wasn't wearing any pants.

Fuck, he thought. *That's one hot honey bucket...*

"Then you *do* know this is a spaceship, right?" Charity asked.

"Yeah," Snowie said. "We figured that out pretty dang quick once I tried on these funky sunglasses. I put them over the camera on the drone too, so's Dawn could see, but then the battery up and crapped out." At this, she slapped herself in the forehead.

"So, the bridles in Crafter's basement are like teleporters, and so are the ones here, and at least one in Manse Lucifer," the Writer, who couldn't have cared less about a lost drone, collated in his head.

"Which means the aliens are in tight with the Devil, right?" Snowie asked.

"Evidently," the Writer replied. "We've been coming across evidence of that all day, but it really doesn't matter, does it? We have to get out of here."

"You know the way out?" Snowie asked.

Charity pointed down the black, buzzing corridor. "Back that way, maybe a hundred yards. Follow me..."

The three of them made brisk strides back down the hall. But, after, say, a hundred yards, there was no sign of the egress through which Charity and the Writer had entered.

"That's fucked up," the Writer said quite elegantly.

Charity said, "It has to be right around here–we didn't walk any farther than that."

"What's it look like?" Snowie asked, unaffected by the fact

that she was bare from the waist down.

"The same shape as the doors in Crafter's basement," said the Writer.

"Only black, just like these walls," added Charity.

"With a large upside-down cross embossed on it."

Snowie nodded. "Same as like me and Dawn saw in the Devil's house! Which is made of heads on the inside, too! Live heads, even in the bathroom. Shit, even the *toilet's* made outta heads!"

The Writer's eyes flicked from Snowie's bare pubis to Charity's heaving bosom. "I guess all we can do is keep looking."

Snowie's tits bounced when she protested, "But there's lots of doors like that in this fucked up place. We go through the wrong one, we might's wind up in Hell!"

"Or on another planet," Charity suggested. "Who knows, with this incredible technology."

Was their new confusing dilemma then interceded by the sound of footsteps?

Yes!

The eyes of the three interlopers went wide. Just up the corridor, four women in black cloaks and hoods and black sunglasses were moving toward them, taking identical steps.

"I think our hosts have arrived," said the Writer. In a rare surge of bravado, he withdrew the big Webley pistol from his plastic bag, held his other arm out, ordered "Stay behind me," and then he aimed the gun at the four women.

"Shit!" Snowie said. "Paulie said some chicks just like that made Augie's bones melt!"

"We saw someone outside with no bones," Charity said. "And we saw two women like that enter this spaceship when it was invisible."

The Writer didn't even have time to lose faith in his big pistol, when–

psssssssssssssssssssst!

–something snapped, then flashed, and a twenty-foot-long

tongue fired out of one of the alien's mouths, and knocked the pistol from the Writer's hand.

So much for the Writer's bravado. "Run!" he yelled.

But the prospect was nipped in the bud when they all turned to flee in the opposite direction.

A luminous black wall stood behind them, blocking the passage—a wall that hadn't been there a moment ago.

"Or, not run," the Writer amended, and they all turned back around.

Now they were trapped. Up ahead, the four women in black advanced, with ludicrous crimson smiles on their radiant, white faces. Charity and Snowie each grabbed onto the Writer, just as the Writer prepared to pee in his pants.

A high and rather girlish voice seemed to resonate from the direction of the black-garbed women:

-hello?-

-hello!-

-don't worry!-

-we're not going to hurt you!-

These statements indubitably came from the four women, yet none of their lips moved. *Well, shit,* the Writer thought. *They're aliens. What could I expect?* "We just wanted to look around; we didn't mean to intrude, or threaten you in any way," he said stupidly.

-oh, that's all right!- one of the women communicated. *-our Supremate has determined that a species as silly, stupid, and weak as yours can't possibly hurt us. That's why we haven't killed you yet.-*

The Writer was waylaid. Supremate? *That must be the boss...* "Could you, uh, please show us to the, uh, exit?"

-the...? oh, you must mean the extromitter- the woman said with what seemed preposterous enthusiasm. *-we'll do that maybe, if you help us with our problem.-*

The Writer, Charity, and Snowie all looked at each other in

dumbfoundedness. "We'd be happy to assist you in any way we can," the Writer offered.

All four of the women squealed in delight, and in such a pitch that was nearly nauseating. But the Writer knew for certain now that these woman weren't really vocalizing. They were using some kind of psychic pulses in place of speech.

-but first,- one of them said, *-we need to take one of you to our lab for a genetic assay.-*

"Whuh, what the fuck's that?" Snowie asked.

The Writer's mouth felt dry. "It's a lab test to determine the components of a person's genetic structure."

"I have a feeling I'm the one they want," Charity said.

-you're right!- exclaimed the lead woman. *-do you want to come with us willingly, or do you want to be deboned?-* From the woman's mouth emerged a long, thin, snakelike appendage with a barb on the end of it.

"I'll come willingly," Charity said after a sigh.

-great!-

Very quickly, two of the cloaked women took Charity by the arms.

"If you don't mind my asking," asked the Writer, "exactly where is your lab?"

-it's right here, or anywhere we want it to be!- exclaimed the lead woman with a giggle.

With that, a previously invisible panel opened in the black wall next to them. It disclosed another hallway, this one lit with orange light. The women led Charity into the passage, then the last of the four turned.

-all hail the Supremate, who exists to serve Satan! wait here for us. we won't be long.- she said.

The panel closed, and they were gone.

"Fuck!" Snowie shouted. "This is some crazy shit! Space chicks that worship Satan? This impossible fuckin' spaceship? And now they've done taken Charity!"

"I'm afraid so," said the Writer, but in spite of the predicament, he found himself gazing fiercely at her bare thighs and palely glistening pubic patch. "By the way, Snowie, I'm sure there are far more important questions I should be contemplating right now, but...why aren't you wearing pants?"

"Huh? Oh, yeah. When that dang second door opened in Crafter's basement and I got sucked in, my pants got sucked in too. I dunno where they ended up."

This sight of Snowie nude from the waist down only amplified his already unnaturally stimulated libido. *I wouldn't mind laying some pipe right now,* he thought in a hot flash. *But I must keep my mind on the business at hand!* "Our next course of action seems pretty limited. We can trust these untrustworthy alien women to bring Charity back and show us the exit, or—"

"Or we can run our asses off and find the exit ourselves!" Snowie elated.

The Writer didn't think that he would actually abandon Charity, but when he turned around to look at the black corridor extending behind them, alas, he saw that another black wall had raised, which left them cut off in both directions.

"That solves that problem," said the Writer.

"Fuck," articulated Snowie.

The situation now had them both standing in a compartment about five feet long, five feet deep, and of an indefinite height.

"Whuh-what now?" fretted Snowie.

"I guess...we wait till they bring Charity back..."

Snowie grabbed at him. "But what if they don't?"

The Writer blinked. "Then...we're screwed. We're at the mercy of hostile aliens..." He was surprised by how calm he was upon arriving at this supposition.

"Fuck. They was taking her to a *lab!* They're probably doing experiments on her! And when they'se done, they'll do experiments on *us!*"

The Writer considered the possibility. *They can do whatever they want with us,* he realized. *They're probably toying with us. They'll probably kill us...*

The look in Snowie's eyes let on that she realized the same thing. Then she sort of fidgeted where she stood and said, "And, fuck! I'm horny as hail–er, I mean I'm *always* horny as hail but what I mean is, shit! All of a sudden, I'se hornier than, like, *ever!*"

"I am as well," he admitted, his erection agonizing in his pants. "Charity said she felt the same thing too. There's something about this place, something in the atmosphere of this ship or whatever it is. It's triggering our sexual responses, causing undue libidinal stimulation–"

"Yeah, and it's makin' us wanna fuck!" Snowie added.

"My impression is that it's a deliberate symptom of this vessel. In other words, these aliens *want* us horny..."

"You mean, they *want* us to fuck each other's brains out?" Snowie figured.

"I suspect so."

"But why? You mean they'se pervs and like to watch humans get it on?"

"Could be, but more probably it's part of their design to study the reproductive functions of other species," he acknowledged, "which must be for an utterly diabolical purpose."

"Why diabolikural?"

He looked right at her, in dead seriousness. "Because these aliens are also *Satanists.*"

By then, as if you hadn't already guessed, that steeped, heady atmosphere of arousal had begun to dump more sex hormones into their brains and, subsequently, their groins. All of the Writer's monitors of civility ceased to operate. In the next instant, Snowie was squealing as the Writer primitively yanked her shirt up.

Those tits! he thought. *Those tits!* and his hands were all over them with no prelude. Each hot, bulging orb of tit-meat pumped in his hands like a massive pair of hearts.

At just that moment, his psyche seemed to ignite. Like a diamond bullet fired right into his brain (where did *that* come from? *Apocalypse Now?*), the most precise and razor-sharp notion occurred to him, and that notion was this: that "tits" were the most magnificent things in the world. Whatever it was about them–mere sacks of fat covered with skin and topped by nipples–that catalyzed such a profound reaction in men... well, the Writer approved of it very much.

Without conscious effort, he found himself pressed right up against Snowie, squashing her with his body while his hands continued to accost her boobs. She, with a big dopey grin on her face, wasted no time in reaching for his crotch, even as she hauled one of his hands off her tit and shoved it down into that flourishing nest of yellow-white pubic hair. In no serious expenditure of time, his finger popped into the soaking groove to diddle around to its heart's content. As with the hand on her tit, his finger could feel her pulse, which felt frantic.

Next, she unceremoniously hooked her mouth to his and began to suck on his tongue. This sensation alone (one with which he was not particularly well-versed) nearly caused him to jettison his next appropriation of semen into his pants (an event with which he *was* well-versed of late), and before he knew she had opened his pants, leaving his erection with no choice but to throb in anguish against her belly.

"Shit, Snowie," he groaned. "We're gonna have to do something about this. It's against my better judgement, but–"

"Shit on yer better judgement!" she wailed back. "We'se probably gonna die on this stupid spaceship, so let's fuck before we do!"

For a change, the Writer found no flaws in her perspective; in fact, it seemed a postulation of pure logic. "But-but you could get pregnant," he managed to voice a dwindling concern.

She gave his crotch a more deliberate squeeze. "Naw, I

cain't get knocked up 'cos I get a quarterly depo shot from the county! It's free!"

This gave the Writer means to reflect. *Depo-Provera, the progestin-based birth-control treatment, highly effective...*

And so came the end of his "reflection." She was right. What difference did it make anyway? Of all the things that could happen to them in this predicament, death had to be the highest statistical likelihood.

"Okay," he said. "Here goes..."

He pulled his pants down. He didn't have to pull hers down, of course, because she *had* no pants. Suddenly there came to him the idea that they stood in a coffin on end–the way those front and rear walls had risen up once Charity had been taken.

The Writer felt Snowie's hand exploring his recently freed erection and, as if surprised, she remarked, "Dang! Never realized it was this big!"

The Writer leaned back and looked down and he, too, was surprised. *Holy fuck! Where did that prong come from?* because the erection that his groin now sported was bigger–*much* bigger– than the one he'd been used to for his entire adult life. *Fuckin' thing looks almost a foot long!* Not that he was complaining, mind you, but there had to be a reason for his organic mirage. *Of course! Whatever manner of libidinal stimulant they've got going here, I must be hallucinotic. It's making me THINK my dick's much bigger than it really is!*

Yes. That had to be it.

But...if that were the case, then Snowie must be having the same hallucination, delightedly jerking it around like a stickshift. "It's like a tool, ya know? A big fuckin' *tool!* It belongs in a tool box!"

Enough of this silliness. The Writer reached behind and lifted her up by just under her thighs, such that the opening of her vaginal entry (a.k.a. her South Mouth a.k.a. her Meat Sleeve) hovered just above the throbbing tip of his newly enlarged erection (a.k.a his Zipper Sausage a.k.a. his Trouser Mauser).

"Actually, Snowie, that's exactly where it's going now, into *your* tool box."

And with this affirmation, he lowered his hands, to admit the entirety of his hard-as-a-rock cock into her nether realm, yes, into that swampy, precious inlet of her womanhood...

* * * *

Perhaps I'm mistaken or perhaps not, but I suspect many of you are too young to have been around in the days when Intermissions were common in movie theaters.

Typically these pauses were engineered in the middle of exceedingly long motion pictures (over two hours, say). I recall many such instances during movies my parents (God rest their souls) took me to in the '60s. Movies like *The Longest Day* (great movie about a crucial historical event but–oh!–it was *three motherfuckin' hours long!*) *The Sound of Music* was three hours long as well (and you really have to wonder if Christopher Plummer was humping Julie Andrews silly between takes). Let's not forget *Doctor Zhivago,* you guessed it: three motherfuckin' hours long, oh, and *Lawrence of Fuckin' Arabia,* which clocked in at 222 minutes!

Now, I'll be the first to admit that these movies were important, and they made important parts of our history more accessible to the masses. Ah, but when you're six or eight years old, you don't know the difference between Doctor Zhivago and Doctor Seuss, and nothing could be more mind-numbing than Lawrence of Fuckin' Arabia. I didn't know what it was about when I was fuckin' seven and I *still* don't. Some dull horseshit about the Ottoman Empire. What were they the emperors of? Ottomans? The things you put your feet up on in the living room? Some empire.

Anyway, it was movies like these that made kids in the '60s

VERY GRATEFUL for Intermissions in the theater. It gave young punks like me time to get our asses out of the seats, run around, and raid the concession stand for Three Musketeers, Neccos, Chuckles, and all that great stuff (and those caramel cylinder-things with the sugar paste in the middle!)

There was also an exceedingly long movie called *Battle of the Bulge* that came out in 1965 and choked at the box office like the Americans choked at Pearl Harbor. (Dwight Eisenhower even came out of retirement to pan the movie as laughably inaccurate.) It was re-released in theaters in 1968, so my wonderful parents dragged me to it. By then I was eleven years old, and I was starting to notice something of a "battle of the bulge" going on in my pants, and I was becoming *very* interested in the cute concession girl who would sell me Chuckles. Damn, I still remember that cutie-pie after all these decades! (As a side-track, I'll mention a movie in the '70s called *A Bridge Too Far,* about a famous World War II battle that took place in Holland. Critics absolutely reveled at this title, calling the flick *A Movie Too Long.* And not only was it painstakingly long, it was about a battle in which the Allies got their asses handed to them! Who wants to see that shit?)

Oops, sorry. I'm digressing. I was talking about intermissions during long movies, and the reason I bring that up now is to serve as an intermission from *this fuckin' novel.* The truth is simply that *I* needed a break from it myself. (Additionally, I *refuse* to write another sex scene, so I'm going to pull the cop-out move and, yes, leave it to your imagination.)

Damn, where is that cute concession girl when I need her? And where's my pack of Chuckles?

* * * *

Snowie leaned exhausted against the luminous black wall, tongue hanging out and eyes showing mostly whites. "Fuck! Ain't never been fucked that good in my whole dang life! And– shee-it! Lookit all that nut you put up me!"

The Writer's larger-than-it-had-ever-been cock slid out of Snowie, limp but still fat as one of those Hillshire Farms sausages. In fact, if anything, his dick was bigger now than when he'd plowed it into her!

Of course, since they were both still standing up, its removal effectuated a very viscid downward exodus of semen that seemed to reflect an amount that could be called far more than copious, even preposterously so. *Damn!* thought the Writer. *Did all that come from me? This damn spaceship's turning me into Superman...*

"What a great orgasm," Snowie murmured. She wrapped her arms around him and just hung on him as if he were a phone pole. "Why'n'cha git yer dick back up'n fuck the daylights out of me again?"

The Writer could only stand upright due to the support of the black wall that had popped up behind him. "Because I'm OLD," he answered, "and I'd have a heart attack even trying. Besides, we've got more important matters to deal with. Like what happens if those women don't come back with Charity? Are we going to be sealed in this cubicle forever? Shit. When my book gets released, will I be alive? Will I even be on this planet?"

Instantly, however, as if in answer to his concerns, the front and back walls of the "cubicle" vanished, and Snowie and the Writer collapsed upon one another. He stuffed his dick back into his pants, then groaned as he climbed to his feet. When he'd helped Snowie back up, he couldn't help but notice that globs of his semen were *still* dribbling out of her vagina.

Back among them were Charity and two of the women in black.

-hello!-

-hello!-

"Uh, hi," said the Writer.

-we're happy to tell you that our genetic assay of your friend was successful,- one woman told them. -and it yielded promising results, confirming details crucial to our agenda.-

166

The Writer, however close to death he might actually be, could not let this opportunity escape him. "Ah, yes, your agenda... Well...Miss, if you don't mind my asking, what exactly *is* your agenda?"

Both women looked at each other, giggled, then said at the same time: *-our agenda is to ruin all intelligent life on this planet by contaminating the native population with multiple hybrid species derived from the flawed lifeforms of other planets.-*

Here the Writer was thrown for a big loop. *What the fuck?* "Oh, I see... But won't that take a long time?"

-of course!- said one woman. *—thousands of years! but the Supremate doesn't care! he's immortal!-*

The Writer raised a finger. "Then since you're not adverse to responding to a few questions, we couldn't help but notice a number of decidedly occult symbols in this... this place. On Earth these symbols are indicative of the worship of Satan. Is this correct? Do you worship Satan, the adversary of God?"

A humming pause filled the luminous air. *-of course we worship Satan, as we exist to serve the Supremate who is a vassal of Satan!-*

The Writer, then, couldn't resist. "So you also believe in God?"

-of course we believe in God! to deny the existence of God is to deny the existence of Satan—a heresy!-

The Writer nodded. "I see. But you can understand that, as a man from Earth, it strikes me as peculiar that aliens such as yourselves would also be *Satanists.*"

This time both women looked at each other again, paused for an unnecessarily long period of time (like characters in a David Lynch film), then both exploded into the loudest witch-like cackling laughter yet. *-we're not the aliens! YOU'RE the aliens!-*

Guess I should've seen that one coming. "Ah, yes. From your standpoint, I can understand why you'd see it that way. So, anyhow, now that you've finished your genetic test, what about us? You did say you might let us go...if we helped you with something. Now I can assure you, we're all too happy to assist you in any way. What can we do for you?"

One woman stared dumbly, then seemed to recollect something, and said, -*oh, yes! that! we came back here to survey one our of hybridization trials from the past, and our sensors indicate that THIS being here-* and at this the woman touched Charity's shoulder -*is a by-product of those experiments...but she only represents half of the field order. we're most interested in the other half, the twin sibling of this woman, and our analysis of some local verbal discourse indicated that this other half is referred to as "the bighead."-*

Charity looked at the Writer. "I think they want the Bighead for further analysis. They want to refine its genetics so they can reproduce it by the millions, to let loose on Earth. And they want to see what happens. They want to see if all those Bigheads would take over the planet."

Like the Engineers in the Alien movies, realized the Writer. *Wow, what a ripoff.* "If you don't mind my asking, then, why exactly would you want that?"

The two women in black giggled again. -*to wreak murder and atrocity over all, because it is the wish of the Supremate who exists solely to serve the will of Satan!-*

Ah, so THAT'S it, realized the Writer, with a long frown. *Devil-worshiping aliens who've got nothing better to do than wipe out humanity. Of all the stupid, unoriginal things!*

-*if you help us capture the bighead,-* the woman continued, -*we'll let you go unharmed. If you don't, we'll subject each of you to slow, agonizing genital torture, but you will not be permitted to die.-*

"Great," said the Writer. "We'll take option number one."

Both women in black giggled with glee; it was like the fluttery cheeps of a massive number of canaries. One woman inserted her upside-down cross into a keyhole in the black wall and—

SWOOSH!

–they all were standing in a luminous black ante-chamber, facing a doorway-shaped opening though which the swamp could be seen, along with the abbey in the distance.

"This is the same place where we entered," Charity observed.

Snowie stared out, mystified...then she scratched her public hair.

"Their technology, no doubt, allows them to traverse great areas of space in the ship, at a whim and a moment's notice," the Writer offered.

-we'll be waiting here for you,- said one of the women, *-and we'll leave this ingression point open. please deposit the bighead here once you capture him. he can be dead or alive, which ever you prefer-*

The Writer's face appreciably lengthened. "Well, uh, aren't you, um, going to help us restrain him once we find him? You know, with your superior alien technology?"

-no!- the woman blurted. *-we already tried that, and several of our sisters got their arms, legs, and heads pulled off. the bighead is immune to our spicules, so we're unable to paralyze him, and we can't dissolve his bones or exsanguinate him.-*

"Well, I hate to tell you this...ma'am," the Writer went on, now a bit peeved. "Even with Snowie and Charity helping, we can't possibly overpower the Bighead and bring him to you—not on our own!"

-oh, so you've changed your minds? you'd prefer slow, agonizing genital torture?-

"No!" he, Charity, and Snowie all replied, and then the Writer continued, "What I mean is, ma'am—considering that the Bighead is huge, homicidal, and possessed of superhuman strength, it's going to be a very difficult task for us to bring him to you without us getting killed."

The woman's garishly shining lips smiled, and she replied, *-take it or leave it. and please don't demonstrate the extreme stupidity of your species by trying to escape us. we traveled thousands of light years to land at this precise point. we'll be able* *to find you in moments, and if you force us to go to that trouble, your punishment will be even worse than eternal genital torture. we hope you understand.-*

The Writer gulped and nodded. "Understood. Come on, girls. Let's get started." And then he, Snowie, and Charity stepped through the oblong doorway into the fog-filled swamp.

-good luck!- bid the two women in black, giggling. *-we'll be right here waiting for you!-*

The Writer and his "team" waded through the sickly fog toward the shore.

"Fuck," Snowie said. "We're fucked."

The Writer nodded. "I'd say that assessment of our situation is correct."

"Then all we can do is run..."

"Why bother? Them nut-job women are right. They'd recapture us in two seconds and we'd probably die worse than any other humans in history."

-oh, we forgot to tell you,- one of the women in black called after them. *-don't stand in that swamp fog too long. it's the exhaust gas from our energy systems, and can cause mutations!-*

"Now they tell us!" yelled the Writer. The trio ran for the shore, the Writer wondering if he'd have a heart attack in the process.

"So, now what do we do?" Snowie complained. "There ain't no way we're capturing the fuckin' Bighead!"

"I know," said the Writer. "But we have to try." He looked over at Charity, who seemed unaffected by the indubitably grim situation. "Well, you sure look cool, calm, and collected, Charity, considering we're about to get mashed to pulp by your brother."

"This situation isn't as impossible as you think," Charity said, glancing up at the abbey's bell tower.

Snowie scratched her ass cheek. "What'cha mean by that?"

"Yes," said the Writer. "I'd be very interested in hearing any tactical or strategic analyses you may have formulated."

"Come on," Charity instructed. "We need to go inside the abbey..."

Since the Writer had no real abilities in management and guidance, it struck him as logical to follow Charity's lead. After all, she'd been to the abbey before, and for over twenty years she'd honed her instincts to keep herself alive and well in the woods, with no help from the modern world. The three of them jogged out of the fog-filled swamp and marched up the incline toward the decrepit building.

Dusk had now fully fallen. Strident night-sounds of crickets and peepers flowed about them, and the darkness between the trees soon filled with the shifting green lights of untold fireflies. They circumvented the abbey, then Charity stalked right up to the front wooden double door, pushed through it, and walked inside like she owned the place.

Let's not forget, also, that the Writer was still lugging around his plastic Safeway bag, which housed the Webley revolver, a remaining bottle of Collier's Civil War Lager, and (of all the previously-unmentioned conveniences!) three penlights to aid them in their trek through the dark building. Charity led the way, swaying her light beam back and forth, followed by Snowie, who kept her beam on the dusty floor, wary of holes, while the Writer kept *his* beam on Snowie's perfect, milk-white ass.

Through another set of doors, they entered a dark chapel strewn with garlands of cobwebs; from everywhere drifted the smell of mildew. "This looks like it here," Charity said.

"Looks like what?" queried the Writer.

No answer ensued, as he and Snowie followed Charity to a corkscrew staircase just behind the old choir screen. First, she, then Snowie, then the Writer all awkwardly ascended this unnervingly wobbly staircase. The Writer managed to divert his attention from their rising height by keeping his light trained on Snowie's butt, enthused that her higher elevation to his vantage point afforded him bull's eye view of the bottom of her vagina showing through the glimmering white pubic tuft. *What a wonderful world of imagery!* he mused.

A hinge keened, and suddenly moonlight tinted them: Charity had pushed open a trapdoor through which they climbed into the covered bell tower, the curiosity of which was increased by the fact that it no longer possessed a bell.

The Writer leaned over the rail and gazed out over the endless expanse of nighted woods. "So what's the plan now? We stay up here and keep a lookout for the Bighead?"

"No, I'll do that," Charity said. "You still have that pistol, right?"

The Writer nodded, and withdrew the big revolver from his bag. "Right here."

"I'm sure the Bighead knows we're in the vicinity," Charity said. "He and I have kind of a psychic bond from our alien genes." Then, quite abruptly, Charity stripped nude.

Mama mia, thought the Writer once he got an eyeful of those big tan tits sticking out. "I'm not complaining but...why did you take your clothes off?"

Charity shrugged. "It just seemed appropriate. The Bighead's a hybridized psychopathic sex maniac. Seeing his twin sister *naked* will only entice him further."

The Writer supposed she had a point. "Well, okay. So what do Snowie and I do?"

"First, fire one shot in the air. That should get Bighead's immediate attention."

"And then what?"

"Go down and hide in the woods. If my plan works, we'll be all set, and I'll be able to deliver the Bighead to the spaceship. If my plan *doesn't* work, then you'll probably see my arms, legs, and head fly off this church roof fairly soon. And if *that* happens, then run for your lives. Or, probably better, kill yourselves, unless you want those women to have their way with you."

The Writer didn't bother frowning, but he did say, "You do realize, don't you, that even if your plan works, we'll be assisting the aliens in their ploy to wipe out the human race, right? We're selling out our species in exchange for our own lives."

Charity flapped a hand in disregard. "Yeah, but that won't happen for thousands of years. Why should we care? In a thousand years, there won't be anything left of this planet. Wars, plagues, pollution, global warming. Shit."

"Yeah," Snowie added. "Won't be anything *left* for those dumbass aliens to wipe out, so we might's well do this."

Okay, thought the Writer, and took a last look at her adorable naked pubis. Then he raised the big Webley pistol, cocked it, and–

BAM!

–fired a shot in the air as instructed.

"Whoa!" he yelled when the gun nearly bucked out of his hand. The concussion was ridiculous, and his ears were ringing.

"Go!" Charity yelled. "Go hide!"

The Writer and Snowie clattered back down the stairs, rushed out of the church, and went to hide in the nearby woods.

From their position below, Charity could be seen in considerable detail, for the big moon and cloudless sky provided a perfect backdrop. The Writer gazed more intently up at this heroic woman, and felt a surge of admiration. "She's volunteering herself as bait, against an unstoppable, inhuman adversary..."

"Yeah, but there ain't no way she can capture the fuckin' Bighead," Snowie said. "What this *plan* of hers?"

"I don't know, and I can't imagine what it could be." The Writer continued to stare upward at the nude woman's imposing silhouette. "Earlier, she did mention something about a secret weapon..."

"A secret weapon?"

The Writer nodded. "All we can do is wait and see."

Snowie moved over closer to him. "And did you– Did you..."

"Did I what?"

She giggled. "When she took off her sundress–fuck! Did you *see* the pussy on her? I mean, it was *ginormous!*"

You don't know the half of it. The Writer cleared his throat. "Uh, yes, Snowie. I did happen to take note of that." Of course, he *didn't* elaborate upon any "elbow-deep" details. "She has similar genetic markers to the Bighead, and I guess it just worked out that they share the same *genital* features. Bighead's got a giant penis, she's got a giant...a giant..."

"Oh, I get it," Snowie said and giggled again.

"Apparently, twenty some-odd years ago, the Bighead raped Charity, but she didn't die as any other woman would have."

Snowie's eyes opened in wonder. "I reckon she's the only gal on Earth who can take all of the Bighead's junk, on account of that *ginormous* pussy on her."

"Precisely," the Writer affirmed, "and spoken in true erudition."

Snowie smiled and took the Writer's hand. "Speakin' of pussies, your jism's *still* dribblin' out of mine." She squeezed his hand tighter. "And I *like* it..."

"I'm edified in knowing that, Snowie. Now, why don't we focus on our current situation?"

She nudged him, then ran a hand over his crotch. "Come on. Fill me up again for the hell of it, huh? My pussy needs to be *beat up* by your cock!"

"No! I'm too old!"

"Aw, no ya ain't." Her hand slithered around more urgently over his crotch, feeling for the zipper tab. "Lemme take it out'n play with it. I'll bet'cha I get him interested–"

Before he could object further, they both jumped in startlement at the sound of Charity whistling. The loud, piercing sounds shot out like the shrieks of a bad bearing; she was whistling with two fingers in her mouth, you know, the way boys do (a feat that this author was never able to accomplish as a boy, and of course, now, I'm so fuckin' *old* that I don't remember even *being* a boy!)

Several more of the ear-piercing blasts fired out into the night, and then Charity shouted at the top of her lungs: "Hey! Bighead! Here I am, so come and get me! I know you want me! I know you can't stand the fact that I'm still alive! So now's your chance! Come and kill me, brother!"

The pitch and volume of Charity's rant was nearly like that of a trumpet, and in its aftermath came an echo that must've traveled for miles.

Then, silence.

Some time lapsed, then. How much? Who knew? At some point, the Writer and Snowie both sat down in some brambles behind a mammoth oak tree. Both were clearly nervous–few wouldn't be–and both kept their eyes glued to the silhouette shape of Charity stalking back and forth on the abbey roof. The Writer thought of a metal duck in an old carnival shooting gallery, back and forth, back and forth.

Eventually, Snowie sidled over against him and fell asleep. Her bare legs lay still and spread, and in a wholly unnecessary and blatantly sexist observation that has no legitimate place in a novel, the Writer found himself intrigued by this image of her spread legs, her pubis, and her colorless clump of public hair shining like spun silver in the moonlight. Monet could've painted such an image; Van Gogh, too. Imagining their reinterpretations thrilled him.

However, in spite of the severity of the situation (and very much like the unnamed protagonist in Lovecraft's "The Lurking Fear") the Writer also found himself struggling to stay awake. Even as he reasserted to himself the importance of remaining vigilant, indeed, he dozed off, and found himself delightfully afloat in the cradle of a dream of rolling green hills and meadows, a gentle baby-blue sky, and myriad bunnies milling about and eating grass. *They're just the cutest little things!* the Writer thought in the dream.

Now, here is where I will steal from Lovecraft, because I'm certain he won't mind as he rests in peace.

The dream of bunny rabbits snapped and it was out of phantasmal chaos that the Writer's mind leapt when the night grew hideous with shrieks beyond anything in his former experience or imagination, for in that shrieking, the inmost soul of human fear and agony clawed hopelessly and insanely at the ebony gates of oblivion. He awoke to madness and the mockery of diabolism, as farther and farther down in conceivable vistas that phobic and crystalline anguish retreated and reverberated.

Thank you, Mr. Lovecraft!

Finally back to his senses, the Writer recognized only an empty space beside him that should've been occupied by the pants-less and big-titted Snowie. Yet more hideous shrieks whirled round his head like crows encircling dead prey. Adrenalin punched through his half-awake confusion as well as the lofty shouting of Charity who was bellowing down from the roof.

"Wake up, you dick! He's gonna kill her!"

It was then that the Writer came back to full, heart-shuddering wakefulness, and he looked up to see the screaming Snowie being kneaded like dough in two inhumanly large hands. Resisting with all her might proved one-hundred-percent useless, as those giant hands slowly and even teasingly positioned her bare crotch (which was liberally voiding urine) over a prong of an erection that was *two feet long*, coursing with snakelike veins and draped with horrific foreskin.

Of course, the two hands belonged to the Bighead, which the Writer's sense of vision verified immediately. Though he'd already seen the Bighead in a sense, seeing him now, like this, about to bust Snowie open with his monstrous cock, this added a new dimension to the situation, a dimension of incalculable, unreckonable, and utterly helpless horror. Something in the

Writer's mind would not allow him to take in the vision all at once; instead, only quick glimpses were permitted: a glimpse of the Bighead's huge malformed head, the one baseball-sized eye, and the other marble-sized, now fully regrown. Eight feet tall, nine feet? What did it matter? It was a mass of pallid, sluglike skin, grayish brown with sickly dark yellowish patches. Could the breadth of the creature's shoulders really be five feet, or had the horror of it all merely amplified the Writer's already ravaged imagination? Muscles seemed to grow over more muscles, all flexing under the swathes of skin which shined as if oiled.

"Don't just stand there!" Charity yelled down. "Use your gun! Aim for his eyes!"

Yes! Yes! thought the Writer. *I've got to do something...*, and in a blind second he'd raised up the Webley revolver, and in another blind second—

WHAP!

—the Bighead slapped it out of his hand.

Now essentially only semi-sentient, the Writer tried to stand fully upright, but was unable to due to the almost physical force of the Bighead's sheer *stench*. No quantity or quality of adjectives could communicate to you the potency nor the tenacity of its effect, and not even the finest Lovecraftian adverbs could modify those adjectives in a manner that would put you in true possession of its nature. The Writer, of course, gagged as if being asphyxiated, and his eyes teared up from the ammonia-like component of the monster's netherworldly body odor.

By then, Snowie had passed out and her machine-like screams had ceased, such that she hung off of Bighead's hands like a half-nude redneck ragdoll. It was clear that the Bighead knew the Writer was watching; it kept looking down at him with that huge gross-out eyeball the color of raw oysters, and the great fang-crammed mouth smiled cunningly. Then the beast took a broad step forward, which brought it into the moonlight and backlit the scene into crisp silhouette. Certainly, the monster was getting ready to rape Snowie with deliberate slowness, all for the sake of protracting the Writer's horror.

He's gonna kabob her with his dick and there's nothing I can do to help! he realized. He patted around feebly on the ground, hoping to find the pistol and save the day in the final second, but the gun was as lost as all his other hopes and dreams. And just as the Bighead would ram his unthinkable erection into Snowie's hayseed vagina and thereby rout her innards and tear her organs from their seats—

That crisp moonlit silhouette of the Bighead and his prey disappeared, blotted out by the much larger shadow of something standing *behind* the Bighead.

At this point, reality collided with the phantasmagoric and the utterly impossible, to form a perfect union. It was like a moving linoleum block print or a nightmare movie image from a German Expressionist director. As that larger shadow moved and shifted angles, the Writer could make out what it was, and when the realization finally smacked home, he collapsed back to the ground and could only stare upward at what was happening.

This sudden larger shadow, indeed, bore a *human* shape but no human could be twenty feet tall, could it? Nevertheless, this shape, this twenty-foot-tall *thing,* grabbed the Bighead by the throat and flung him with little effort into a massive tree. There was a great, reverberant *THUD.* The Bighead, in all his power, terror, and glory, let out a groan like a large beast in pain, like an ox or a rhino, a groan of dread.

Its mysterious twenty-foot attacker stepped more solidly into the moonlight to reveal itself in detail...

Un-fucking-believable, thought the Writer through the clots of his stupor.

It was a naked woman.

That's right. A *twenty-foot-tall* naked woman.

And I can further delight to tell you that she possessed a total brick shit-house body, like the chick in that 1985 sci-fi vampire film called *Lifeforce.* Fuck! Remember her? I forgot her name, Matilda Something. It was directed by Tobe Hooper, I think.

Anyway, that's the kind of body this buck-naked twenty-footer had. As well as long brownish hair like Charity that went down past her knees. However, as she stalked closer to the bewildered Bighead, the angles and positions of her movements did not quite afford the Writer a glimpse of her face–at least not until–

The Bighead straggled up to stand but he did so waveringly, his giant monstrous hands perceptibly shaking. It may well have been that this infamous creature of local legend was experiencing *fear* for the first time in its life, and with good reason, because–

WHACK!

–the giant woman backhanded the Bighead across the face so hard that the big eyeball flew right out of his skull, and a good many of his wolf-like fangs jettisoned from his mouth.

Holy shit, thought the Writer. *She's kicking the Bighead's ass!*

Not that there was much left to kick, not without teeth and minus an eye. The Bighead roared in a leonine fashion, perhaps to intimidate his attacker...but there was none of that. The giant woman trounced right up to the Bighead (those massive yoga-ball sized tits joggling spectacularly), reached down with a hand three times larger than the Bighead's and–

Will you be surprised to hear it? Probably not!

–tore the Bighead's cock and balls right out of his groin.

The Bighead collapsed, outraged, and curled up into a fetal position, mewling like a sick walrus. The woman, who may have chuckled just then, lobbed the Bighead's massive and infamous junk lackadaisically into the woods, all that terrifying meat shrinking in defeat. All the vaginas that had been busted open by it, and all the innocent women who'd died, were now avenged.

Charity looked down from the roof of the abbey. "Great job, honey. I'm so proud of you. Now, would you please take him down to the swamp and leave him in front of that weird thing that looks like a doorway?"

The hulking figure nodded, and with no effort at all, flung the still-mewling Bighead over her shoulder, and walked him down to the swamp where the invisible spaceship was waiting.

The Writer immediately tended to Snowie, who'd been dropped right before the scuffle. *Thank God!*

She was just coming to on the ground. "Whuh-what the hail happened?" she asked.

"I'll tell you later!" said the Writer, with more than a little exuberance. "Thank God you're all right!" He kissed her on the mouth and–well–yes, gave one of her boobs a good old-fashioned sexist squeeze.

"Not a bad plan, huh?" Charity said. She was still standing on the abbey's roof, naked, feet apart, hands on hips, her great mane of hair jostling gently in the night breeze. "And the best part of all is, we won't have to suffer eternal genital torture now!"

We're home free, thought the Writer with a long sigh.

"Look!" Snowie exclaimed. She was pointing down to the moonlit swamp and the strangely lit doorway that seemed to exist in midair. "They'se draggin' the Bighead into the spaceship!"

That they were. While the twenty-foot woman stood aside, several of the those nutty women in black dragged the Bighead's shuddering body into the doorway. One of the women looked up toward the Writer and waved.

It's all over, he thought, and could scarcely believe it. *And over so fast.* It was almost anti-climactic. *The giant naked woman bitch-slaps the Bighead, knocks his eyeball out, pulls off his cock and balls, and now he's already loaded into the spaceship. That's it? That's the end of the legend of the Bighead?*

He couldn't believe it, but it was so.

"You've figured it all out by now, right?" Charity asked from the roof. "My secret weapon?"

The Writer's fabulous mind ticked, then slugged to a halt.

"Well, no. How did you get that twenty-foot woman?"

"She's my daughter, of course. I already told you, over twenty years ago, the Bighead raped me..."

The Writer's eyes widened. "And the product of that rape... was that giant woman..."

"Exactly. The Bighead impregnated me all those years ago. My daughter's father is also my twin brother; that's some pretty screwed up incest. Anyway, her name is Annabelle, after my Aunt Annie." Charity called down to her bodacious twenty-foot daughter. "Come on back up, Annabelle. I'll introduce you to my friends."

Narration will have to suffice for this next segment because...well, because it's easier. After the Bighead was hauled into the invisible spaceship and the ship's door disappeared, the naked twenty-foot woman–"Annabelle"–re-scaled the incline and approached the Writer and his coterie.

Need it be said that the footfalls of this extraordinary woman actually thudded the earth such that their vibrations could be felt by the onlookers? *That is one BIG piece of ass,* thought the Writer in a daze as he examined her outline during her ascent. Irrelevant abstractions sailed around his brain. The yoga-ball sized breasts were one thing, but further contemplation forced the Writer to consider the following bit of deductive reasoning: *Charity is her mother. And Charity has a REALLY BIG vagina. So if Annabelle is four times bigger than her mother...isn't it quite possible that Annabelle's vagina is four times bigger than her mother's?*

Ah, these purposeless (though very interesting) suppositions must end here and remain unanswered.

She reached them, whereupon Charity properly introduced her, and explained how she and Annabelle had been living their lives in the forest, quite satisfactorily, these past two decades. Now that the "Bighead" saga was over, they would both return to that self-same forest.

A moment later, Snowie (who was, of course, still pants-less) pointed with urgency to the swamp. "Holy fuckin' HAIL! Look!"

To be sure, something was afoot. The Writer suddenly found himself looking at the most impossible sight of his life (yes, even *more* impossible than the sight of a twenty-foot-tall naked woman)...

The spaceship had turned off its guise of invisibility, and was now visible to any eyes that could see it. Something like a vaguely luminous, jet-black Empire State Building sitting upside down in the middle of the swamp, only much bigger, a mile high at least. A rising pressure could be felt in everyone's ears. The fog in the swamp began to glow overtly, more fog pouring out of exhaust vents on the object's sides. Next came a loud *POP!*

And the spaceship was gone.

"So much for the aliens," said the Writer.

"Fuck 'em," Snowie said. "I hope they crash."

"All in a day's work!" Charity chuckled.

"Let's go back to the house and celebrate," suggested the Writer.

As they proceeded to do this, the Writer discovered that he had a new point of vantage as far as Annabelle was concerned. Previously he'd really only seen her as a back-lit silhouette, but now the moonlight shone full on her face.

No, it was not the face of a hybridized monster, nor the ghastly product of genes run amok. It was a beautiful, creamy complected, high-cheek-boned face that anyone would instantly think of as pretty, except for...

Except for her eyes.

One eye was huge, the size of a soccer ball. The other was tiny (for her), not much bigger than a plum.

Charity took note of the Writer's observation, and nodded and smiled. "Yeah. She has her father's eyes."

EPILOGUE

Annabelle, of course, did not join the group back at the house, simply because she was too fucking *big* to enter.

But the Writer, Charity, and Snowie did enter, and found Dawn safely installed downstairs in the basement, where she was continuing to send the second drone in and out of Hell in order to generate more video footage. It was her idea to post the footage on fuckin' Youtube and get multiple millions of views. WOMAN MAKES VIDEOS OF HELL! NOT FAKE! EXPERTS BAFFLED! That sort of thing.

The Writer, tiring a bit of beer, resorted to raiding Crafter's impressive wine closet, which contained not one single bottle less than a century old. *Today we rid the town of the Bighead and we rid the world of maleficent aliens. Work like that warrants a good drunk...*

All details were related to Dawn, whose big tits continued to print monumentally against her Army t-shirt. She was, of course, fascinated by the exploits of the day.

And—don't forget—Paulie Vinchetti's corpse continued to hang on the spiked bridle door, while another door's spike remained occupied by the corpse of Pastor Tommy Ignatius.

"I think you've gotten enough footage of Hell by now,

Dawn," the Writer said. "It's time we shut down this operation." He yanked both paling corpses off their supernatural spikes, and the two wide open doors on the wall slammed shut.

They all repaired to the upstairs living room to shoot the shit, by which time the Writer had chugged half a bottle of Chateau Lafite 1787 which he determined to be "Not bad, but I'll take a good eight-dollar bottle of Taylor Marsala any day."

Anyhow, the story proper ends here, and there is little need to relate with any detail what else would happen that night, a night which, due to understandable fatigue, they would spend in the house.

I will add that Snowie, remained pants-less. And one more interesting thing did occur before they all went to sleep.

When the Writer was well into a second bottle of wine, (an 1846 Amontillado, possessed of an intriguing "nose" and an absolutely ethereal polish of nuts and aromatic herbs), Snowie and Charity both excused themselves–at the same time–for the bathroom. The Writer, being fairly shit-faced by then, thought nothing of it, and instead found himself leering at Dawn's boobs, as she'd already fallen asleep on the richly carpeted floor.

What a fuckin' RACK! It just keeps getting better and better!

Well past midnight, by the cozy glow of a single Depression-era hanging-head lamp whose intricate glass-mosaic shade seemed to depict the return of the Prodigal Son, Snowie and Charity came back into the room, both seeming simultaneously part sheepish and part triumphant.

The Writer glanced groggily up from the couch. "Hi, girls. You both look like you've got something on your minds."

"I sure as shit do," Snowie stepped forward and announced, her bare pelvis front and center. "When me and Dawn went to the store earlier to buy the drones, I bought somethin' else too. This." She held up a little white plastic thing.

Naturally, the Writer asked, "What's that?"

"It's a EPT, a early pregnancy test, the latest kind," Snowie said. She showed it to the Writer. A little circle on the plastic stick had two red lines in it. Snowie beamed. "The 'structions say two red lines mean you're preggo!"

Dawn, who'd woken, burst out laughing. "He's gonna be a daddy?"

Fuck this shit! thought the Writer. "This is bullshit!"

"The hail it is! Ya fucked me in the spaceship and ya fucked me the other night when we was doin' them creampie videos for Paulie."

The Writer's lower lip depended. "But-but...you said you were on birth control, the quarterly depo-provera shot!"

"Yeah, I know! Got my last shot four months ago, but I guess it didn't work."

The Writer sat up on the couch, outraged. "That's not quarterly! *Three* months is quarterly!"

Snowie frowned. "But four is fourths and fourths is quarters..."

"No, no! *Three months* is quarterly, damn it!"

"Oh, shee-it. I thought...well, ya know. Whatever," Snowie dismissed. "Don't matter no how. There's a bun in my oven and it were *you* who put it there."

Then Charity took a step forward and held out another plastic test thing that had two red lines on it. "And I hate to tell you this, but *I'm* pregnant too."

The Writer's eyes bugged. "Not by me, you're not! My sperm never got anywhere near your vagina!"

Charity shrugged. "After I jerked you off on my tit and rubbed my hand over it, I may have stuck my hand in my vagina when you weren't looking. Presto!"

The Writer seemed to deflate on the couch, and he couldn't help but think of the line from Ecclesiastes that described women as "more bitter than death."

"Don't worry," Charity said chirpily. "I won't require very much child support, and you can have joint custody!"

Terrific, thought the Writer, and started chugging more wine.

"Hey," Dawn blurted. "He creampied me the other night too! Gimme one of those EPT's!" She took it into the bathroom. A moment later she squealed in glee. "Jackpot! He knocked me up too!"

(Yes, yes, *please.* I realize that EPT's don't work that fast, but often in books and movies you must sometimes suspend your disbelief for the sake of the story!)

The Writer went on to finish the current bottle of wine and put a big dent in another one before he completely passed out.

And this is where the story, essentially, arrives at its conclusion.

The Writer, in his newfound wealth, would shortly thereafter buy the Crafter house, which he got for a surprisingly modest price from the bank. It seemed as good a place as any to settle down.

Of course, Dawn and Snowie would live there as the bundles of joy in their bellies got larger and larger, while Charity and Annabelle would retreat to their preferred abode (i.e. the great outdoors) but did stop by on a regular basis. For such occasions, the Writer had a barn built close on the property where Annabelle could sleep, since she was way too fuckin' *big* to fit in the house.

But I'll mention only in passing that the diligent reader need not assume the saga is fully completed.

Remember, though the Bighead is long gone, his cock and balls are still sitting out in the woods someplace, and I suppose that some unwitting character in the future—say, a hunter, or, better, a creeker girl—might find those monstrous genitals and put them to some arcane use that might make for an interesting bit of fiction.

Additionally, I'll remind all those readers with less than exceptional memories or attention spans that only *three* of the Larkins quadruplets have met their Maker. Those would be

Horace, Clyde, and Gut. If you'll recall, the fourth brother, Tucker, had headed *east* in search of Horace's murderer, and has not been mentioned again. Perhaps he will pop up at some future time, to carry on the entertaining traditions of the Larkins Clan...

During the weeks following the climax, the Writer also contemplated, without much success, his next book. He supposed what obstructed his creativity was the anxiety that went along with the knowledge of three babies on the way that had all been sired by his sperm.

He'd never had dreams of fatherhood and had never even considered such a circumstance. *I'm a recluse novelist, not a daddy!* Even in all his mustered positivity, he couldn't think of any way to look at the situation with satisfaction. Changing diapers was *not* his forte, nor was making goo-goo gaa-gaa noises at drooling, chubby-faced babies. One afternoon, while sitting on the front porch, taking in the view of the unkempt witch's graveyard to the left–and drinking–his cellphone rang. His expression drooped when he saw the UNKNOWN NUMBER on the screen.

"You again," he muttered into the phone. "What is it this time?"

"Hey buddy bro!" his doppelganger enthused. "Just calling to congratulate you on making it out alive. Great job when that giant bitch took care of the Bighead and packed his ass off on the spaceship, huh?"

"Yeah. Great job."

"And you get a big high five from me for knocking up all three of those fuck-pigs in one swoop. Not bad work for an old man!"

"Yeah, not bad."

"You'll be able to open yourself up your own Tom Thumb day nursery! Your very own baby ranch! Just think of all the *shit* those little crumb-snatchers will be producing under your roof!"

The Writer nearly swooned with the thought. "Gimme a break. The situation is depressing enough without your commentary."

"Why depressing? You're not seeing this from the bright side, brother. Just think of it. When Snowie unloads hers, it'll be a kid with your genes mixed with *Lovecraft's!* How cool is that?"

Something along the lines the Writer seemed to recall having contemplated before, but only theoretically. Now, however... *Hmmm...*

"Now that you mention it, that *is* pretty cool."

"Damn right it is! And when Charity pumps hers out, it'll be a kid with your genes mixed with the *Bighead's!*"

The Writer stared blankly into the woods. "Well, that's not quite as cool..."

"Oh, sure it is! You'll be the father of an alien monster! Now *that* sounds like fun! And then there's Dawn. When her kid hits the deck, it'll be your genes mixed with...a redneck hosebag's! Just hope it's a girl. Think of the *tits* it'll have when it's older!"

The prospect set the Writer to chugging more beer.

"Anyway," the doppelganger continued. "I just wanted to let you know that I'm almost done with our next book."

The Writer's eyes narrowed. "Oh, really? Don't you think it would be nice if you let *me* write one?"

"Hey, face it. You're too old now and burned out. And you're gonna need all your energy just to raise those three kids."

"I'm not *raising* them!" the Writer blurted. "I'm just paying. Snowie, Dawn, and Charity'll be *raising* them!"

"Don't kid yourself, bro. Those three bimbos are out the door the minute those babies crawl out of their joy-holes."

"They wouldn't do that!" the Writer felt sure. "They wouldn't *abandon* their own kids—"

The doppelganger laughed so loud and uproariously that the Writer nearly fell from his chair.

"Trust me, those sausage jugglers will be fucking *everything that moves* while you're here neck-deep in baby shit and paying the bills they rack up on *your* credit cards. Get ready for it, my friend. Welcome to the real world!"

The line went dead, and all the Writer could do was sigh.

But it only took a few moments before he began to see through all his lackluster interpretations of life and instead behold a great big beautiful world looking back at him: the blue sky, the venerable trees, and myriad birds drifting on errant breezes. And more than that: the promise of a new future.

It's not that bad, right? So what if I have to change a few diapers and raise a few squalling, pain in the ass kids? I'll bet I even enjoy it. It's something new. It's not the same old story, and one thing is for sure. I'm ready for THIS story to be over...

Just then the phone blipped. It was a text message from–yes!–an unknown number, and the text read as thus: THE STORY'S NOT OVER 'TIL I FUCKIN' SAY IT IS.

ABOUT THE AUTHOR

Edward Lee is an American novelist specializing in the field of horror, and has authored over 50 books. Lee is particularly known for over-the-top occult concepts and an accelerated treatment of erotic and/or morbid sexual imagery and visceral violence.